BLISS

a novel by

ELIZABETH GUNDY

The Viking Press   New York

c . 2

First published in 1977 by The Viking Press
625 Madison Avenue, New York, N.Y. 10022
Published simultaneously in Canada by
Penguin Books Canada Limited

LIBRARY OF CONGRESS CATALOGING IN PUBLICATION DATA
Gundy, Elizabeth.
  Bliss.
  I. Title.
PZ4.G9729Bl [PS3557.U483] 813'.5'4 77-21721
ISBN 0-670-17431-9

Printed in the United States of America
Set in Linotype Palatino

The lyrics on Pages 205–206 are from "I Know a Friendly City" by
Irving Caesar. © by Irving Caesar. Used by permission.

BLISS

Dangerously depressed stringbean
spinster-professor, 34, finds life
dramatically changed by the village
ditchdigger.

Each spring brought thoughts of suicide.

It began with the first warm winds of March and peaked in April when the thaw began in earnest, flooding the valley with the scent of new life.

She walked along the campus with her head tucked forward, eyes down, avoiding encounters. It was time to take off her woollies; that would make a world of difference. There was no need to jump off the knoll by Vincent Hall and make a mortal splash about a simple sultry breeze.

What was desire anyway? Just a biological function distorted by myth. She dragged her feet. And wasn't it natural that the season of birth should call up thoughts of

1

death? Thoughts of nothingness. A wave of longing passed through her, and a shiver of fear. It was worse this year, this terrible fascination. A broken piece of pavement ended the meditation.

"Careful, lady."

She looked up with a self-deprecatory laugh, mocking her own clumsiness before anyone else could. But the man merely gave her a friendly smile, showing a missing tooth, and turned back to his digging.

They were digging everywhere, destroying sidewalks, repairing stairs, painting what needed painting, workmen in plaid shirts, heavy vests, knit caps; for a moment, the scent of blossoms and earth was crossed with a rich male fragrance. She climbed the steps of the English building and made for her class.

A few of the students were there; she waited for the others, opening her briefcase, taking out books and papers.

"This is our last meeting before exams, so if there's anything you'd like to go over . . ."

Chaucer. Shakespeare. Shelley. She knew it all by heart, could conduct a class speaking Middle English if she had to, could deliver a lecture without faltering, could write a learned article on any number of great dead men, but when it came to the live ones . . .

She knew it was unfair to blame everything on her looks, but after all being so tall did present definite problems. There were, she was sure, women who could make six foot one work for them, larger-than-life goddesses. She was a larger-than-life stringbean.

Beauty was skin deep; that's what they said. Only her homeliness had its beginnings in her marrow. Why else should large dark eyes, no more than moderately deep-set, look as though they were trying to hide themselves from the world? Her teeth were even, small and white; so why, when faced with a strange situation, should she smile as though she

BLISS

were apologizing? As for the rest of her face, it was pale and narrow, and she hated it.

In spite of everything, she achieved a certain chic, the only one possible for her frame, an angular elegance set off by Scottish tweeds, made to measure by mail. And of course there was her voice, a husky seductive thing, a gift bestowed on the wrong person. Once, as a student in journalism class, she'd been assigned to interview a soon-to-be-famous politician. He'd been cordial on the phone, more than cordial, asked her to meet him in a restaurant. The look on his face when she approached his table still repeated itself in her nightmares.

Sometimes she thought she should never have entered academic life but instead become a telephone operator and married a nice blind man.

"No more questions? . . . You may leave early then." She put away her papers and books, clicked her briefcase shut. "And have a good summer."

Chairs were pushed back, notebooks closed.

A student approached her desk.

"We got a lot from your course, Leona."

One or two in every class . . . young girls who developed crushes on her, seeing in their teacher's raw-boned limbo something manlike but harmless.

No doubt she should have been a lesbian. She read articles in feminist magazines by women who found the relationship satisfying. She read articles about masturbation; she could write a book on the subject.

The ten-of bell rang, calling her to devotion, only it was her three o'clock class instead of prayer, and a university, not a convent. If nuns could cope with springtime so could she. . . . She shuffled down the hall to her office. The window was open, and the April air filled the room, its breezes ruffling the papers on her desk, rattling the venetian blinds, playing with the posters on her wall.

3

Both were travel posters of whitewashed thatch-roofed cottages smothered in ivy and flowers. Behind their tiny latticed windows—she smoothed the paper down with her hand—her secret self lived, in other centuries, with Shakespeare, Donne and Herrick.

The real window, with its vernal scents and suicidal suggestions, was an intrusion and a threat. She walked over to draw it closed. The men below were on their break, leaning on their shovels, drinking tea from plastic thermos mugs.

Among the rough crowd, she noticed the man who'd spoken to her: dark green cap over shaggy hair, massive shoulders in plaid flannel. He finished his tea and wiped his lips with the back of his wrist; as he raised his arm, the white cuff of winter underwear peeked through.

She really had to put her woollies away tomorrow.

The man with the green cap and an older man beside him took out tobacco and rolled cigarettes, bending over their shovels to light their matches in the wind.

They struck match after match but seemed to have no success.

The younger man laughed, an ignorant gap-toothed laugh. His ears stuck out, making him look slightly moronic.

The older man leaned toward him. "Better give me a light from yours, Bliss."

She smiled to herself. What a ridiculous name for such an oaf.

Hazel heaved out of her rocker and put another chunk of birch in the stove. She adjusted the draft and peeked into the oven. Bread browning.

Uh oh. Commercial over.

Back she slapped across the linoleum in her rubber sandals, settling again in the rocker with a bag of potato chips.

Young Tony Andrews appeared on the screen, sitting with his head in his hands.

"What's the matter, Tony?"

"I don't know."

Hazel chomped.

"Is it something to do with Emmeline?"

"You know I love Emmeline."

Hazel nodded her head.

"And there's nobody else?"

"I can't explain it," said Tony. *"It's come over me all of a sudden, the strangest feeling . . ."*

His face grew big in the TV screen, and the organ music rose.

Hazel stood up and flapped to the cupboard, took out a bottle of premeasured formula.

"I found a picture in your dresser, Flora."

"A picture in my dresser?"

The baby suckled in Hazel's lap.

"A picture of young Tony Andrews."

The shed door banged, and the kitchen door.

"I'm home!"

"Take your boots off." Hazel didn't turn from the TV screen.

"I did a good drawing in school today."

"Teacher hang it on the wall?"

"Here." The child shoved it in Hazel's face.

"What's that?"

"Trees and horses."

"Did teacher say it was good?"

Janie nodded.

"Put it on top of the TV then." Hazel got to her feet and laid the baby in his crib, leaning the bottle against his teddy bear.

"Can I have some hot bread?"

"Get out the butter if you want some." Hazel set the loaves on racks, brushing their tops with melted shortening.

"Smells delicious, Mommy."

Hazel sniffed. Delicious was right. Didn't it take honorable mention up to the Sourgrass Fair?

Sourgrass was the nearest village of any size. Not that

Fingabog Siding wasn't a village too. It had a post office and a school to grade six, but there wasn't hardly a hundred souls lived into it, and it didn't even have a siding. Freight trains passed by, but they never stopped no more.

Oh, she guessed she liked Fingabog good enough, though she'd rather live up to Sourgrass or, if the truth be told, smack in Town, high on the hill near the K-Mart, with a lawn and a picture window and a husband who worked in a bank.

She sliced off a piece of bread and spread it with butter. Tom Flagerty worked in a bank. She thought he liked her too, out in back of the church hall that time. "Here's your bread."

Janie grabbed the bread and stuffed it into her mouth. "Can I watch Sesame Street?"

"Go out and play." Camilla Starr was supposed to have an abortion at four o'clock.

"I don't want to go out."

"Shush." Hazel settled into her rocker.

"*I can't go through with the abortion, Miles.*"

"Can I watch Camilla, Mommy?"

"*You'll go through with it.*"

Janie crept over to her mother and sat down on the linoleum.

"*It's murder.*"

Hazel nodded.

Miles clenched his hand in a fist.

Janie reached up her hand and put it inside her mother's.

"*I'm not afraid of you any more, Miles.*"

"Good girl," said Hazel.

Miles's fist moved toward the TV screen, and the organ music rose.

"Can we watch Sesame Street now?"

"Shush."

Miles came back on the screen, shaking and frothing at the mouth.

Hazel rocked in her chair. Drugs was a terrible thing.

"Mommy, we learned a new song in school today."

"I have to have a hundred dollars."

Janie raised her voice. " 'Oh Canada, glorious and free! We stand on guard, we stand on guard . . .' "

"I guess I got to bath Joey"—Hazel sighed out of the rocker—"and get your father's supper."

" 'Oh Canada, we stand on guard . . .' "

Hazel undressed the baby and put him into the plastic tub, soaping his soft fat body while he splashed and made gurgling noises.

She couldn't gripe too much. She had it pretty good to what she could have if she married, say, Cousin Eddie, who she always thought to marry. There was Eddie's woman in a tarpaper shack, with no lights, no running water, not even no TV, and kids popping out of her as fast as he put them in.

Just the same as Mum and Dad.

Mum never had nothing, not even no washer. Hazel looked at the sun shining in on her washer. She'd soon have a dryer too; she was working on it now, a real pretty one she seen in the catalogue, avocado, just nine-fifty a month.

She gave the baby a little tickle. Good job she didn't marry Eddie, still be living in Burnt Mill, without no telephone or stores or neighbors. Neighbors was a comfort. A person could look out their window here and see more than a hill of cows.

She patted the baby with talc and pinned him into his diaper.

"Look, Mommy."

Hazel turned to the TV. Big-tailed birds strutting around, flashing their feathers like fans. Land, wouldn't it be pretty in color!

"Peacocks," explained Janie.

"Be nice in color, wouldn't it."

"Can we have a color TV? Huh?"

8

She put the baby back in his crib. "Ask your father."

"I'm going to show Daddy my picture first thing."

"Let him take off his boots before you do." She raked the embers forward and put in two more sticks of wood. "I don't want him tracking the floors."

"Think he'll like my picture?"

Hazel sliced potatoes. "Lord knows."

"Think he'll hang it up?"

"No telling."

Potatoes was awful scabby. For what a person paid these days, they sure didn't get tit for tat. "Where you going now!"

"To meet him."

"Don't you run out without your clothes on!"

Janie was gone, boots unlaced, no jacket, no sweater, banging through the shed, into the muddy yard. Hazel looked out the window.

Janie was in her father's arms.

Potatoes not even fried, and I never washed them dishes from lunch.

"Hello, Hazel."

"Lo, Bliss."

"I did a picture for you, Daddy."

He kissed the back of Hazel's neck as she bent over the sizzling potatoes. "Good day?"

"Never enough time."

"How's Joey?"

"Look, Daddy."

"Well now." He held the picture up, turned it around.

"The other way."

"Horses, ain't it?"

"Teacher said it was good," said Hazel.

"We better hang it up then." He tacked it to the wall, alongside the two calendars from the two shops in Fingabog Siding.

9

"You want to see Joey?" Janie led her father to the crib.

"Hiya, kid." Bliss swung his son in the air.

"Looks cute, don't he?" asked Janie.

"Yup."

"And I looked just like him, right?"

"The very same."

"You had a bit more hair," said Hazel, stirring pea soup on the stove.

The baby pulled his father's ears.

"You think they're handles, eh?"

"Daddy, can we have a color TV?"

"No."

"It's only twenty a month," said Hazel.

"Nothing wrong with what we got." Bliss let his son dribble on him.

"For animal programs."

"Look," said Janie.

They turned to the TV, where some cats were gobbling Purina.

"You can see cats in any color you want next door to Mabel's." Bliss chuckled. "Ain't that so, Janie?"

Hazel sliced the cabbage. "Joey's due for a checkup."

"Seems like we just took him."

"Can you take off one afternoon?"

"Maybe."

"What about Friday?"

"I'll ask the boss."

She'd have to buy the *Courier* Thursday and check the sales, take out the pink and press it; she hoped it hadn't grown too tight. She'd put on quite a bit of weight with Joey.

"Can I come?" asked Janie.

"You got school."

"I always got school!"

10

"Don't whine." Or I can wear the yellow. The yellow's plenty roomy.

"It ain't fair," said Janie.

"Set the table."

"I never get to Town."

"It's just the doctor's," said Bliss.

"It ain't just the doctor's." Janie set the plates out. "You'll go to the K-Mart too."

"Come get your soup."

"Maybe I'll be sick Friday, and then you'll take me to the doctor's too."

Hazel passed the potatoes around. "You'll know the reason why if you're sick."

"Lovely weather," said Bliss.

"I never got out." Hazel blew on her soup.

Janie started to sing. "Let's go K-Marting at the K-Mart . . ."

"Eat your potatoes!"

"There was a breeze from the south all morning." Bliss crunched his cabbage salad. "I'd hate to work in an office in weather like this."

"Not as though you could," said Hazel, "with sixth-grade education."

"I might've ended up custodial."

"That ain't office."

"It's indoors. Same thing."

Hazel slurped her disagreement via the pea soup.

"Suppose I was really sick?" asked Janie.

"I seen some crocuses," said Bliss.

"Did you!"

"In front of City Hall."

"They won't be up here for a month."

"You never know with this fine weather."

"The mud's hard on the floors is all I know."

"I'd sure like to take a day off and go fishing."

She could let the seams out on the pink. And Mabel could run it up on her sewing machine.

"Not that I will," said Bliss.

"Can I come fishing with you, Daddy?"

"Ain't going fishing."

"Can I go to the K-Mart with you Friday?"

Pink is more becoming than yellow. "Stop messing with your cabbage, Janie!"

"I seen a groundhog, Janie."

"Where'd you see him?"

"On the side of the road. Standing up like he was waiting for to catch a bus."

"Show me how he looked, Daddy."

"Something like this."

She'd take the pink to Mabel's tomorrow, give her lots of time to sew it good. "Pick me up a box of hair-perm on your lunch hour, Bliss."

It was spring of course, her fatal enemy, inflaming her beyond reason or logic, whispering to her beneath its gentle breezes that tonight, perhaps tonight . . .

"Leona!"

"Hello, Dolly, glorious weather, isn't it?" Leona trailed after her hostess like a giraffe behind its trainer. She rarely went to parties. She saw enough of her colleagues at meetings, in the cafeteria, at the library, at the bank, at the supermarket, too much of them. Still, tonight . . .

She'd done her best with herself. She was wearing the heather suit and the beige silk shirt which opened at her throat, showing her collarbones. She'd put on smart uncomfortable shoes instead of oxfords. Her skin was scented with Sikkim. She'd brushed her light-brown hair until it shone; more was impossible because her hands were inept and she refused to go to beauty parlors after coming out several times looking like a floor lamp that someone had topped with a frilly boudoir shade. Now it hung as it always did, unswervingly vertical, lopped off midway down her interminable neck.

"Taste one of these sandwiches, Leona. Sandy Coverly sent them over, and everyone says they're out of this world." Dolly Chiasson fluttered off to greet someone else, and Leona picked up a sandwich, nibbling at it with interest, as though cheese and watercress were the real purpose of her appearance at the party.

Was there anyone in the room she didn't know? Any mysterious stranger? . . . She knew them all, the men with their politics and their theories, and the pretty pampered women.

Most of the women wore long, soft, slinky skirts and old-time starlet hairdos, which waved and dipped around their faces. What would it be like to have a face like Dolly Chiasson's, with cheeks like glistening petals and a mouth like a smiling bud, and a ripe little peach of a body?

She ate the out-of-this-world sandwich. To feel oneself all gentle curves instead of angles, to know it was enough just to exist, to give pleasure to the world simply by being there.

The men were something else. They were her colleagues, ambitious, conceited. No, she wouldn't want to be a man. The voices tinkled and rolled, light and heavy voices, touching, clashing, mixing, reaching out to each other.

"Leona, how good to see you. Come say hello to Muriel."

"Grand to see you too, Peter." Peter Wilson—Milton scholar, said to be next in line for department head, if he could topple the incumbent. He swept her into one of the sparkling groups.

"Did you see the latest at the Playhouse?"

14

"Terrible, wasn't it."

"Sylvia's review was on target for once."

"I thought she went rather far, making such a to-do about Keith McKeith's lack of sex appeal."

"Keith thought so too. He went to her office next day and attacked the poor girl."

"Successful?"

"Let's face it, the level of theatre in New Brunswick . . ."

"Why Keith! No show tonight?"

"Dear Deirdre got laryngitis."

"Wouldn't that be an improvement?"

"Alistair's emptying his pockets. I'm afraid he's going to stand on his head again."

"He insists it prevents hangovers."

"It looks like he's going to give an inverted speech."

"Just as long as he doesn't give his *Gunga Din*."

Leona found herself doing the thing she despised most, joining in the flippant chatter.

"Where's Finnamore this evening?"

"He's under the knife, isn't he?"

"He's in hospital, but they won't carve him up till tomorrow."

"I see Margaret's consoling herself."

All eyes turned to the end of the room, where Margaret Finnamore was talking to Basil Holland.

An appreciative chuckle ran through the group, for what woman could be interested in Poor Basil?

Well . . . one woman. Leona's heart had always gone out to that ugly man on the couch, who had an excruciating stutter and an inner-ear condition which made him constantly hear the twitter of birds. He'd told her about his affliction over a beer at the Corner Pub. After his third beer, he took the dreamy bloom off her sympathy by confessing that he was queer.

15

"Did you hear Chuck Chiasson's taken to TM?"

"Dolly's frantic."

"He gets into trances and won't even answer the phone."

"Hauffer was into that for a while. His house almost burned down before the smoke shook him out of his spell."

"That wasn't TM, it was opium."

"Get me another drink, will you, Arthur?"

"What an atrocious dress Nadine's wearing."

"I don't know. She looks rather like a Christmas present."

"Theodore's long-awaited *Life of Swift* is coming out next month."

"I've seen the galleys. It's simply . . ."

"Theodore! How good to see you."

She walked away. She couldn't stand herself, went to the drinks.

"Can I help you?"

"Thanks." She smiled down at a swarthy man with a face like a basset hound. He moved his hands gracefully, dropping in ice cubes, whisky, soda. "I'm Ronald Fowler."

"Leona deVos."

"I've seen you in the cafeteria, reading . . . Donne, I think."

"Yes. Donne." Her cleverness had fled, leaving her shy and stupid with a man who'd noticed her. A hound-faced man with graceful hands.

"I'm in the history department."

She nodded, towering above him.

"My main subject is Egypt."

"I've seen the mummies," she said.

"Ah yes, the mummies," he agreed. "It's remarkable how they preserved them. First they . . ."

A bit of a bore. But who was she to pass snap judgments? No doubt on another subject he'd be quite interesting. He's so short, almost a dwarf. So what? He certainly knows a great deal about mummies.

16

She nursed her drink as he spoke. He seemed to take a gruesome interest. It was probably only her own ignorance that made it appear so. His knowledge of embalming was actually astonishing.

"My wife. Anita. Leona deVos."

"Delighted to meet you," smiled the woman, a fragile silvery thing, like lilies of the valley. "Has Ronald been boring you about Egypt?"

"Not at all. It's really wonderful to learn about the mummies."

The Fowlers drifted away, and Leona drifted to the door. She should have been disappointed that the little embalmer was ineligible, but all she felt was relief.

She left the party behind her and walked slowly through the sleeping streets, tasting the cool breeze on her face and legs.

Though the night was moonless, the stars made up for it, dazzling the darkness of the sleeping town. It was a solid, well-kept place, no bums or vagrants to threaten her, no one who didn't belong. Even the few familiar loonies were tucked into their family nests after eight o'clock.

She made for the river.

By the end of the week it would flood. It was already rising. The benches along the embankment were just above the water line. They would soon be covered, along with the trash cans and the picnic tables by the fish-and-chips stand.

She stared at the starlight on the water.

She hadn't had a drink for several months and was feeling a little odd, or perhaps Ronald had mixed it too strong, for she found herself in an area of memory overgrown with cobwebs. Fifteen . . . no, sixteen years ago.

She'd been sitting alone on a bench overlooking a river in Scotland. The charm of the old city had worked on her imagination; even at eighteen, she felt more comfortable with the gentle ghosts of another century than with reality.

17

So she'd put off supper and returning to the youth hostel, basking instead in the ancient vibrations.

"You Swedish?" His voice had been tinged with brogue.

"No." She looked up. "I'm Canadian."

He was ruddy, square-jawed. "Staying at the hostel?"

"Yes."

"They get a lot of foreigners. Especially this time of year. The place is overrun with them."

"It was crowded last night," she admitted.

"Did you sign in yet for tonight?"

She shook her head.

He told her what she ought to see in Edinburgh, told her where she ought to go in Scotland, told her she ought to be careful whom she talked to: You wouldn't believe it, but most men had only one thing on their mind.

"Yes," she said. "I guess."

"That hostel's filled by now."

"Do you think?" It was suddenly dark out.

"It's been filled for an hour."

The hostel cost fifty cents; a hotel would cost God knows what; her traveler's checks were nearly depleted. "Can you recommend a hotel that's not too expensive?"

He curled his lips scornfully. "They'll steal you blind. You can stay at my place."

"Oh."

"Let me carry your knapsack."

"I'll get it." Their hands fought over the knapsack, and hers were as big as his.

"Come along." He swung her possessions over his shoulder, and she walked beside him, trying to show she wasn't nervous, trying to show she knew he wasn't a man with one thing on his mind.

"How tall are you?" he asked.

"Six one."

He let out a low whistle.

"That's stocking feet," she added glumly.

"All muscle too, I'm thinking."

She flushed in the darkness. They wound through the narrow streets, and stopped before a red brick house, with a minuscule fenced-in garden.

"You sure you have plenty of room? I don't want to be in the way."

"Aye."

He had an attic bed-sitter.

"Where will I sleep?"

"Next door." He led her through to a smaller room, with an unmade bed. She had to stoop to keep from bumping her head on the sloping ceiling.

He put her knapsack on the floor. "Give us a kiss." His tongue was between her lips and one of his hands was on her breast.

She tried to get free, but he was stronger than she was, glued between her lips, pulling her down on the rumpled bed. "That's enough," she gasped.

He yanked up her shirt, baring her meager breasts. She remembered movies she'd seen and slapped him in the face.

He punched her back, hard.

She burst into tears.

"What did you expect?" He wrenched down her dungarees. "You smack a person, you get it back."

"I didn't mean to smack you. I apologize."

"That's all right." He was taking off his clothes.

She leaped up to retrieve her own, but he pitched her back down on the bed.

She pulled a blanket up in front of her. Her own nakedness was the worst. His nakedness was nothing, even his awful stiff penis standing out like a guided missile. It was her body that threatened them, her long pale lanky body.

He tore the blanket off her. "You're a big bird."

He was crouching above her.

19

The light bulb hung over his head.

He touched her there. "You're pretty dry."

She closed her eyes. He was kissing her there. How could he do it? The tears rolled down her cheeks. The bright bulb glared through her closed eyelids, he was licking her, wiggling his tongue around her horrible nooks and crannies.

"You don't move much, do you."

When someone asks you a question, you answer. "No," she answered.

He opened her with his fingers and tried to put his penis in. "Tight as a drum."

She was weeping audibly, making stupid sniffling sounds.

He rammed her.

She screamed.

Again.

It was beyond tears now. She was broken, ripped apart.

He was panting, sweating, heavy, stinking, stabbing her over and over.

Was she peeing herself? All that wetness. She'd probably peed herself. What did it matter anyhow, when he'd seen the worst of her, eaten the worst of her, broken the worst of her.

He pulled out with a satisfied grunt, his skin tearing away from hers, and walked out of the room.

She heard water running.

She looked down at the sheets. She hadn't peed herself. "Do you want me to wash the sheets?"

"What?"

"The sheets," she said more loudly. "Shouldn't I wash them?"

He came back in, smiling, rubbing his crotch with a towel. "I want Ralph to see them."

"Who's Ralph?"

"My mate."

She sat with the blanket twisted over as much of her as it would cover. "Will you let me go now?"

"There's no place for you to go."

"I could go to the train station."

He sat down beside her and took the blanket away, fondling her breasts and belly. "Loosen up."

"I can't."

"Do you want to use the loo?"

She nodded her head and got to her feet, a big gawky white bird hobbling into the bathroom.

She washed herself as best she could, avoiding the mirror. Her legs were weak and she was still bleeding.

The front door crashed open. "You up?"

"We've got a surprise for you, Ralph."

There was no lock on the bathroom door. She leaned against it.

"She's in the loo."

"A bird? I'm too drunk."

"That's all right with me."

"There's blood on my sheets!"

"That's what I was telling you."

"Why'd you use my bed?"

"You can sleep in mine."

"I'm going to puke." Boots thudded toward her; the doorknob rattled. "Open up!"

She leaned against the door but was knocked aside.

He entered, looked at her, knelt and puked.

She gazed at the dark river. So Ralph was her second lover.

Sixteen years ago. She'd cried all night, except when her mouth was stuffed with flesh, and afterward she didn't menstruate for a year.

Far off, she heard voices and laughter. The party was

breaking up, scattering two by two, strolling back to conjugal beds and baby-sitters.

She got up, and started for home in the fashionable shoes which pinched her feet.

"Land, it's good to get out." Hazel rolled down the window to feel the air, then rolled it up again to protect her perm.

"Hope we don't have to wait too long at the clinic."

"I don't care." There was the magazines to look at and the other people.

"Great weather."

"Yup." Just warm enough for the pink. Where Mabel let the seams out, you could see a dotted line, but the pink sure did set off a person's skin, if she was dark with nice curly black hair.

Too bad the Chevy didn't look a bit more stylish. It was two-tone-like, the topside being blue and the bottom half red-brown, the color of auto putty. Course, it only cost a hundred dollars. Bliss was knacky with a car, always tinkering under the hood; he could make a worn-out Chevy last them thirty thousand miles.

"Embankment's flooded," he said.

"So long as the bridge ain't."

" 'Twon't be. Not enough snow this year." They coasted down the hills which led to the bridge. "You can go to the Trust Company first, Hazel."

She sighed with satisfaction. She liked to put the two dollars in their Christmas Club herself. It was just a thing she liked to do. It had nothing to do with Tom Flagerty, who worked in money orders, maybe seeing her and saying how do, maybe noticing her new perm.

He wasn't handsome, Tom, but he wore a suit with thin white stripes and manicured his nails. She glanced at Bliss's nails, on the steering wheel. A man who worked outside collected dirt, and that was that.

They rode across the bridge; the smokestacks on the opposite side spewed a hundred percent pleasure into her nostrils.

Joey opened his eyes. "Joey's glad to be in Town, ain't you, sweetie?" Hazel tickled her favorite child under his chins.

"Parking lot's flooded," said Bliss. They parked a little ways down.

"You stay with your daddy," she told Joey, straightening her jacket, patting her hair, stepping out onto the sidewalk, click-clack, click-clack up the street to the bank.

Is he here? she wondered, getting on the longest line, behind a woman in a black blazer, rich-looking buttons onto it.

There! Coming out of the back. She smoothed her dress. He hasn't caught sight of me yet. He will. The pink's so bright.

Look at that, would you, a new suit, tan. And his side-burns all gray and curly. Talk about distinguished! Bliss's sideburns don't have nothing distinguished about them.

He was looking her way. She gave him a sociable smile, showing both dimples.

He was walking toward her. "How do."

"Fine. How are you?"

"Lovely day." He was passing on, how-doing others. A person who worked in money orders got to know everybody.

She moved forward behind the lady in black. Now that was a coincidence, running into Tom Flagerty. She'd have to tell Bliss. Not that Bliss knew him, coming from different villages as they did, but he knew who he was. Everyone knew Tom Flagerty, selling money orders.

Out in back of the church hall that time, when he really seemed to like her, if she'd got pregnant that time. Lord, that would have been a stroke of luck!

She handed her book to the girl behind the cage, who filled it in, another two dollars closer to Christmas.

The girl behind the cage was wearing her nails quite dark. It seemed to be the style. Hazel never painted her nails, nor her face. She'd never got started, being Pentecostal and all.

Bliss didn't even know what he was. *Christian*, he said. *That ain't no religion*, she'd answered. Well, he took her to wrastling sometimes, and that was almost like church. Hazel put her book back in her bag, and walked outside. She missed church, but there wasn't no Pentecostal congregation in Fingabog Siding.

"Guess who I ran into?" She got in the car, taking Joey from his father.

Bliss edged out of his parking place.

"Tom Flagerty," she answered her question. *"Lovely day,* he said."

"I see the fish-and-chips is under water."

"He was wearing a new tan suit."

"Supermarket lot's under."

"This dress still feels too tight."

"You've put on a lot of beef."

"I don't need you to tell me."

"It suits you."

"No it don't."

"It does, Hazel." He turned onto Woodward Street. "There's more to hold."

"Don't you be fresh."

The clinic lot was filled with cars.

"There'll be a long wait."

"It's the weather," explained Hazel. "People like to get out."

"The trout'll be leaping."

She got off in front of the clinic with Joey, and let Bliss drive around back to park.

"Have a seat, Mrs. Dawson." The nurse smiled at Joey. "He's big, isn't he."

"Like his father." Hazel found herself a couch, next to an old lady with bandages on her eyes, and laid Joey down in his plastic lounge.

Quite a few pregnant women, six other babies, a couple of crippled-up old folks, two women about Mum's age; she wondered what they was there for, no bandages or nothing. Probably wanted an outing was all.

"Hi." Bliss came stomping in, in his old plaid shirt and patchy pants, with her so nice in her pink. She made room on her couch. An awful pretty purple dress that woman's wearing. Maybe she'd find the pattern and Mabel could run it up.

"Have a magazine." Bliss handed her a *Redbook*.

Some women sure had it good, on every page, with new furniture and a dryer. She'd have one by next winter or know the reason why. It was really this past winter she could've used it, for diapers. After Joey there'd be no more. They wanted a boy and now they had one. She asked Dr. Ross to tie her tubes, but he said not till the third. Well, there wouldn't be no third. She wasn't going to be like Mum or Cousin Eddie's wife, poor all her life for kids.

Bliss rolled himself a cigarette.

Hazel looked up from her *Redbook* at the people coming and going. Dark nails was sure the thing. A person could live and die in Fingabog Siding and never know what color people was wearing their nails. But Joey was a lot fatter than the other babies. Be a bruiser like his father. She looked at Bliss, coughing over his cigarette. An expensive habit, tobacco. In a year, it would pay for a dryer.

"Mrs. Dawson, please."

Hazel picked up her baby, and walked into the doctor's office.

"What are you feeding that monster?"

Hazel beamed. "Just formula and cereal."

The doctor hefted Joey, weighed him, measured him, gave him a shot. "He's certainly a specimen."

She beamed some more. A specimen. I must tell Bliss.

Joey pulled the doctor's glasses off.

"Hey there, young man!"

"He's a cutup," said Hazel.

The doctor recovered his glasses. "Bring him back in a month or two."

Hazel hung around in the doorway. That was the thing about a healthy baby, nothing to ask. The whole exam only took five minutes. "Maybe you think he's too big?"

"No such thing," laughed the doctor.

Hazel dimpled. She liked to see someone laugh at something she said. It was more sociable.

"Bye, big fellow."

"Say good-bye to Dr. Gibbons."

Joey was carried out in silence.

Bliss got to his feet.

"He said he's a specimen."

"Go on!"

"He did." Hazel raised her voice so those nearby could hear it. "*He's a specimen,* he said. *What do you feed him?* he asked."

They trooped out of the clinic and into the car.

"Plenty of time for the K-Mart."

"Anything special you needed, Hazel?"

She took the page she cut from the *Courier* out of her handbag. "Socks on sale and talc and a swamp-coat for Janie. Terry sleepers for Joey, a new pair of thongs for me, electric frypan . . ."

"Ain't we got an electric frypan?"

"This one's round," she said. "Cotton balls, copperized kettle . . ."

"What's wrong with our 'lumium kettle?"

"I just want to take a look. It don't mean I'm buying." Hazel looked out the window. They was driving up the hill, past the split-levels with brick fronting and 'lumium siding, picture windows, clear-across drapes, two-car garages, regular lawns, white storm doors. There it is! Her breath quickened. The For Sale sign was still on it. Still no curtains in the windows. She might buy it as well as the next person.

Bliss steered them into the K-Mart Plaza, working the two-tone Chevy in amongst the station wagons, Dusters, Mavericks.

"Lock the car," warned Hazel. Someone might steal the diaper bag. She carried Joey through the black slush, and waited at the door for her husband.

Sweaters. Pants. Foam pillows. Terry sleepers. Cotton balls. Talc. Swamp-coats. Electric frypans.

"Bliss, get a cart."

Bliss stuck Joey in the cart, and the family wheeled straight forward to the Restauranteria.

The Friday crowd was fairly foaming.

Tammy Wynette was singing over the loudspeaker.

The lights was buzzing.

They bought their tea and found a table.

Hazel took off her jacket, and sat back. In a way, this was the highlight—this little pick-me-up before the serious shopping, sitting under the neon, the three of them, her in her perm and her pink which was still too tight, Joey in his plastic lounge. They chomped on sugar donuts, biding their time, looking nice.

"An awful crowd," said Bliss.

"Quite a few jumpsuits too." She no longer had the figure.

"Why don't you get one?"

"If I see a nice one."

"We ought to get something nice for Janie, for being left behind."

"Like what?"

"I don't know." He rolled a cigarette.

Something was coming back to her. "I got it! Did you notice that girl at the clinic in the purple?"

"No."

"Yes you did. I'm going to get some purple crimpelene and two patterns, and Mabel can run us up a mother-and-daughter dress!"

"Two dresses?"

"One big and one little." Wouldn't they look cute parading through Town together in mother-and-daughter dresses.

"That won't be much of a surprise for Janie, a bunch of crimpelene."

"It's a dress, not crimpelene." She'd set Janie's hair in rollers, both of them so dark; it would be a regular picture.

She shook the crumbs off her dress. They couldn't waste no more time, what with looking over patterns, jumpsuits and everything else. She lifted Joey over the railing and set him in the cart. "Come on, Bliss."

A person didn't know which way to look! There was that much stuff, a lot of it not worth lugging home, but some of it . . . there was the copperized kettles!

Bliss plowed behind her with Joey in the cart. " 'Scuse me, 'scuse me, 'scuse me."

"Wouldn't it make a good wedding gift?"

"Who's getting married?"

"Someone's always getting married." Hazel stuck it in the cart.

Bliss wiped Joey's dribbling mouth.

"Look at them laundry baskets!" She charged off through the aisles. They just didn't last, laundry baskets; it never hurt to have an extra.

"Which color do you like, Bliss?"

"Ain't we got one?"

"Not a bright one. What about this orange?"

"It's bright, all right."

"Shove it under the kettle, Bliss."

She elbowed her way through the crowd. Miracle Slice-O-Matic, as advertised on TV. The very thing she was looking for.

"Ten dollars for cutting your cabbage?"

She made for the center of the store, where the TVs were back to back, every one of them showing Camilla Starr in color.

"What's the matter with her now?"

"Miles is persisting on that abortion."

Bliss sat down.

"You like that Relax-a-lounger, Bliss?" Hazel looked at the ticket. "Ninety-eight dollars, ain't too much."

"I just thought I'd wait for you here."

Also by Elizabeth Gundy

Naked in a Public Place

"I seen them for twice as much into the catalogue."

"What about them patterns, Hazel?"

"You're right!" She steered for the patterns, the cart following after. Mother-and-daughter dresses. That's what me and Mum had. Only with us it was flour-sacking.

The new bulb had no threads on it;
it didn't screw.

The old one had burned out a month ago. She'd sent in a requisition. She'd written a memo. She'd finally gone to the hardware store and bought another one, a long fluorescent tube. But how did it go in?

She could fiddle with both bulbs and the socket, and try to figure the thing out. Only she was afraid that with her clumsiness, she'd electrocute herself.

Or, she could go next door and tell Professor Curdy— Donald Curdy, contemporary prose, with a special interest in women's liberation literature—who'd smile a smile that said *just like a helpless woman*, and make it all right.

Or, she could continue in the dark.

She preferred the dark, but the term papers had taken their toll. Her head was splitting. In another day she'd be seeing double.

She palmed her eyes with her hands. That was supposed to strengthen them. Five minutes with her hands in front of her eyes every day . . . she'd read that somewhere. And carrot juice. But there was nothing wrong with her eyes. It was her bulb. She'd go next door.

She stepped outside her office. There was Curdy's nameplate, and behind the door his voice. He had someone with him. Peter Wilson. Two of them to smile.

She continued down the hall, around the corner, down the stairs. She'd ask one of the workmen to do it; that's what they were there for.

They leaned against their shovels with hard, unsmiling faces.

She approached the man with the shaggy hair. At least she knew his name.

"Would you help me change my light bulb?"

"Me?" He looked up from the cigarette he was rolling.

"It's a tube. A fluorescent tube. It doesn't screw."

"You want custodial, ma'am."

"Aren't you?"

"We're maintenance."

She stared at his shaggy head bent over the cigarette. Maintenance. Custodial. "It's rather a subtle difference, isn't it?"

His eyes met hers, a startling blue, indifferent to the subtlety. "Sorry, ma'am."

She turned back to the building. Curdy it would have to be. Or she'd try again herself. A little shock might do her some good.

"I ain't supposed to do custodial." He clattered up the

stairs behind her, his bootsteps resounding through the quiet hallway.

She let him into her office.

"This is it, eh?" He took the light bulb from her. "Evans's Hardware." He peeled the ticket off. "Don't custodial give you light bulbs?"

"I wrote a memo, but nothing happened."

"Expensive too. They ought to pay you back for it." He stepped on her chair with his dirty boots, and switched the bulbs.

She turned on the light. "That's better."

"I should've put newspaper down first."

They looked at the chair, powdered with dry mud.

"I can brush that off," she said.

He brushed it off.

She opened her pocketbook and held out a dollar. "Thanks for changing the bulb."

"It's all in the day's work."

"Please take it. I realize it's not your job. Custodial . . . or was it maintenance?"

He smiled, showing his missing tooth. "Forget it." His hand was on the doorknob.

"Will you have some coffee?"

"I don't think it. It ain't exactly my break."

She looked at her watch. "It's mine. I'm making a pot."

"You're having some, are you?"

She plugged in the coffee pot.

"I might," he said.

She put two mugs on the desk, Pream and donuts.

He pulled up a chair. "I guess it's almost break time."

She poured the coffee and sat down.

He was looking around the office. She followed his gaze to the posters, the flower-covered cottages where Shakespeare and Donne and Herrick . . .

"I wouldn't want to clean them windows." He pointed to the tiny panes in the photograph.

"Do you clean windows?" She pushed the donuts toward him.

"The wife does, and I hear about it." He gnawed dubiously at the stale pastry. "Did you make these donuts?"

"No. I'm afraid they're not very fresh."

He chewed on the left side of his mouth. His lips were thick, the kind of lips she supposed would be described as sensual. His face was high-boned like an Indian's, but his shaggy hair was gold-brown, and with his blue eyes, the effect was rather striking. Yes, he was handsome. A handsome oaf.

"The wife's donuts took second up to Sourgrass."

"Up to Sourgrass?"

"The Sourgrass Fair. Her donuts took second and her brown bread got honorable mention."

"I've never been to Sourgrass."

"Never been to Sourgrass?" He hesitated, then took another donut.

"I've seen it on the map." She got up and poured him more coffee. She'd seen it on that vague green area she thought of as north boondocks.

"You ought to take a drive there sometime"—he stirred in the Pream—"if only to look around."

"I don't drive."

"You could always take the bus." He chomped. "Or have one of your friends drive you up."

"What would I see in Sourgrass?"

"Well . . . you'd see Sourgrass."

She smiled. "Would I really?"

Her amusement bounced off his blue gaze as off a wall.

"I mean," she said, "is it picturesque?"

"It's quite a size." He drank his coffee. "They got a

hospital and a sidewalk." He looked at her shelves. "They got a library. You could take out a book."

"I'm glutted with books."

"I guess you are." He returned to his donut.

His neck was muscular, and his hands embedded with dirt; black circles marked his nails. He wiped his mouth with his thick plaid shirt.

"Last time I sat down with a schoolteacher"—he took out tobacco and began to roll a cigarette—"was in grade six."

"Is that how far you went to school?"

"Yup."

She figured up her schooling. "I went to grade twenty-two."

"Holy Hannah!" He inhaled deeply and went into a fit of coughing.

"Are you all right?"

"Course I'm all right."

She leaned back and watched him smoke. His plaid shirt was caked with mud and his baggy trousers were patched with six different-colored patches and as many shades of thread. The wife's sewing wasn't up to her donuts.

He fell into another fit of coughing. She saw that he liked to cough; it was part of the smoking ritual.

"You're from somewheres out west, ain't you?"

"Toronto."

"I seen your picture in the *Courier* once."

She'd discovered too late that small-town newspapers send their photographer to anything that could be called an event. Now when she caught a glimpse of the balding man with his cameras at some faculty function, she bolted as fast as her crepe-soled oxfords would carry her.

"The *Courier* didn't do justice," he said, "to the size of you."

She winced.

He coughed. "I guess I better go."

His cigarette was halfway finished.

"Do you have children?" she asked.

"A boy and a girl. We don't have a lot of kids. We'd sooner give just two the benefits."

Leona nodded.

"The wife thinks they need a color TV."

"I don't have a TV."

"No TV?" He gaped at her. "They pay you pretty good."

"They pay me more than I need." She suddenly felt uncomfortable about how much they paid her, more than a man with a family.

"What do you do with yourself without TV?"

"I read. I write."

"What do you write?"

"Books." She corrected herself. "Two books. I'm on my third."

"Stories?"

"Literary analysis."

He shook his head. "Beats me."

She went to her bookshelves and pulled out a volume.

"I don't want it." He motioned it away without touching it. "It's safer on your shelf."

"You don't read?"

"Don't have the time." He looked at his burned-out cigarette. "To tell you the truth, I wouldn't anyway."

She imagined him up in north boondocks, sitting in front of a fireplace, with his son and daughter beside him, and the wife darning his socks. Perhaps they were singing around the piano. She smiled at her greeting-card image of simple family life. "Do you sing?"

He laughed. "I make a noise."

"Do you all sing together?"

"We're not a church-going family. The wife, now, she's Pentecostal, but there ain't no Pentecostal church in Fingabog Siding."

"I didn't mean to ask about your religion."

"Don't matter."

She felt obliged. "I'm agnostic."

"That so? I never heard tell."

"I don't go to church either."

"It's just what a person believes." He went back into his silence. She saw him rummaging there deep among his beliefs. "The wife don't agree."

There was a knock on the door, and Curdy entered. "Can I borrow . . . oops . . . sorry. . . . I wanted your *Reader's Encyclopedia*, Leona."

"Mr. Curdy . . . Mr. . . ." She was fumbling among her books.

"Dawson," said Bliss, rising. He turned to Leona. "If you have any other little job get in touch with me. B. Dawson. You too, Mr. Curdy. Three dollars an hour, three-fifty for car work. I'll do anything but work on the engine itself. Repairs, digging, plumbing, carpentry, masonry, tractors, chain saws." He paused. "There are fourteen things I can do. We counted them up once."

"Well, Mr. Dawson"—Curdy's eyes were twinkling—"for a man who can do fourteen things, I'd say three dollars is fair enough."

Bliss clomped out of the office. His boots thundered down the stairs.

Curdy chuckled. "One of the labor gang doing some moonlighting."

"I don't imagine his salary's much. These men have families to support."

"Absolutely." He continued chuckling. "Quite a character. A decent dentist could make a killing out in some of these rural areas."

Hazel didn't sleep all night, she was that excited.

"Ain't nothing to worry about." Bliss spooned up his Sugar Crisps. "They been here before."

"Not all together."

"You're the one who's doing the favor."

"Why can't I come?"

"Stop your whining, Janie!" Hazel tugged at a hangnail. "I don't want no kids, hear? You go to Linda's house when school's done and don't set foot in this yard till you see them cars drive off." She touched the rollers in her hair. "Do you think there'll be enough cake, Bliss?"

"Enough for a dozen goats."

"I won't make no trouble, Mommy."

"No's no!"

"After," said Bliss, "you and me will have a party with all the leftovers, eh, Janie?"

"But I want to see the Tupperware!"

"Veronica'll leave a booklet." Hazel bit the hangnail off. "If she forgets them paper plates, I'm ruined, Bliss."

He wiped his mouth. "She ain't likely to forget. She's the one that's making the money."

"Only ninety percent. We get the other ten."

"What will we do with it, Mommy?"

"I might get me electric curlers."

Bliss fetched his lunch pail from the counter.

The phone rang.

One two, one two. "It's us!" Hazel leaped to her feet "Yes . . . yes. Four batches of donuts, three cakes, a tub of potato salad. Did you get them paper plates yet? Lord, Veronica, don't forget." She hung up the phone. "That was Veronica."

"I want to see the Tupperware!"

"Come on, Janie. I'll give you a ride to school."

"Don't forget your book bag," yelled Hazel.

The door to the shed banged shut, then the outside door. Hazel gripped her stomach and ran to the bathroom.

This was worse than having a baby, having a Tupperware party. Never again. The cramp passed, but she stayed on the toilet. They say with electric curlers by the time you finish setting your head, it's already time to take them out.

She'd have to wear the yellow; she split the pink at the seams. If she didn't stop putting on weight, she'd end up as big as Mum. Not that it ever stopped Dad much, eleven kids and three misses, enough to drive a woman crazy. She got off the toilet and pulled the flush. There's a sound she never would've heard if she married Cousin Eddie. She flushed it again.

Have to call June and Alva and Mavis and Stella and Lois. She dragged the crib out of the kids' room; she liked to have Joey where she could see him during the day, besides which the TV give him something to listen to.

Nothing but news now. She changed his diaper. A person had to watch the news to keep up, but she didn't favor it. Have to call Theresa and Chrissy and Ellen. And all the Caseys.

She took the bottle from the fridge and sat down in her rocker with Joey. The news would be over soon. Have to call the Hoyts down in the Flats. And the Hunter girls. And Tessie.

Tessie.

Her stomach began to churn again. Should she invite her or shouldn't she?

She had to invite Alva; Alva always bought Tupperware. But Alva with Tessie? Lord, what was a person to do?

She rocked the baby, staring at the news. How would Alva take to sitting down with her husband's girl friend? Specially now with Tessie pregnant, carrying twins, the doctor said.

Hazel wouldn't wish twins on anybody, twice the diapers, twice the bottles. She shifted Joey on her lap.

Course, Alva might not mind, Tessie being her niece and all. Hazel wrinkled her nose. She sure wouldn't want a row, not at a Tupperware party.

She'd ask June's opinion.

She put the baby back in his crib and leaned the bottle against his pillow.

June Setzer had more common sense than a horse. She lifted the phone off its hook.

". . . six dollars for fifty pounds. *What are you selling,* I asked him, *potatoes or pearls?* Oh, I told him."

Mrs. Ives talking. Hazel pressed her ear to the receiver.

"And sugar. Seventy-four cents for a two-pound bag. Sugar, mind you."

Mrs. Sheehan. Hazel plugged her other ear with her little finger.

"Where will it end?"

"No end in sight."

"It can't go on forever."

Hazel moved back to the rocker and settled in for a good listen. Those two old biddies could talk the legs off an iron pot.

"Going to Hazel's this afternoon?"

"It's something to do."

"It's a pastime."

"So long as I get back in time for the story."

"You won't get back for Young Tony Andrews."

"I ain't worried about Tony. It's Camilla Starr that's got me frazzled."

"Awful, ain't it?"

"He almost killed her yesterday."

"They should take him out in the field and shoot him."

"Shooting's too good."

"You're right."

"He got pretty hair though."

"He has got pretty hair."

"Makes me think on how Doug's hair used to be."

"Yes it does."

"Did you notice them plastic flowers on Doug's grave is still pink?"

"I noticed that."

"It's them new ones from Woolworth. They don't fade at all."

"A lot of them a person gets do fade awful quick."

"They ain't made for this climate."

There was silence.

"Did Hazel make her donuts?"

42

"Four batches. I seen her yesterday before supper."

"Think four will be enough?"

Hazel chewed her lips.

"Plus three cakes and a tub of salad."

"Should be enough."

"She makes a lovely donut."

"I really like it more-so than Mrs. Bloot's."

"Well you know why Mrs. Bloot takes first."

"If we was running around with the judge, we'd take first too."

"You don't think nobody's listening, do you?"

"Course not."

"And him with a double hernia!"

"I hear the truss he wears is terrible. Two little bedsprings into it."

"Bedsprings?"

"That's what I hear."

"I never seen it on the line."

"No, they must hang it inside."

"Ain't nothing to be ashamed of."

"Some lines got a lot worse than trusses onto them."

"You seen Stella's Thursday?"

"Was that the day it was so windy?"

"The day she did all them sheets."

"I didn't notice."

"It was between them two mauve pillow slips."

"What?"

"I don't like to say."

"Say!"

"I'll tell you in private. You never know who might be listening."

"But if she put it out on the line for the whole world to see . . ."

"I'll tell you this afternoon, at Hazel's."

"Do you think she's asking Tessie?"

Hazel clutched her stomach and stifled a groan.

"She's got to have Alva. Alva's an awful hand for Tupperware."

"Course, Alva and Tessie are cousins."

"Aunt and niece."

"Is it?"

"Tessie's father's Alva's brother. You know that."

"That's right. If he is Tessie's father."

"I never thought so."

"Me neither."

"Nothing like him."

"She's a Daggett, if you ask me."

"That's what we always thought. That long nose onto her."

"Daggetts run to twins."

"That's right!"

"There you are then."

"Alva and she are still blood."

"Yes, old Mrs. Daggett was a Holmes too, wasn't she."

"So it's almost the same."

"And Alva ain't one for a row."

"I'd take the chance and invite them both."

"Hazel might think different."

"Tessie's always a barrel of fun."

"We better go now. The story's starting."

"Which one?"

"Private Practice."

"I don't follow Private Practice."

"You don't!"

"What's it about?"

"I'll tell you later. It's coming on right now."

The three phones clunked down, and the TV sound went up.

"Is it his heart, Doctor?"

"I'm afraid, Mrs. Wagner, it is."

"How long does he have?"

Oh lands, I didn't get milk for the coffee! Hazel rushed to the bathroom and sat down on the toilet, racked with cramp. Never again! Not for Veronica, not for Tupperware, not for electric curlers. I'd sooner have a wig anyways, one of them new wash 'n' wear ones.

The cafeteria was half empty, and the vacation spirit was in the air. She shuffled to a corner table with her tray.

"Leona used to know him."

She looked up to the next table. "Hello, Peter. Hello, Donald. Whom are you two vilifying now?"

"A friend of yours. You studied under Clem Stegmann, didn't you?"

"He was my thesis advisor."

"Seen his latest?" Wilson picked up a book and pointed the cover at her.

"No, I haven't seen it yet."

"It's not too bad," said Curdy. "Rather flashy."

"Slick as usual." Wilson munched on a bread stick. "But when you get finished, you say so what?"

"Stegmann's always been mostly style." Curdy was sipping wine; he kept his own bottle in the kitchen.

"I'll lend it to you." Wilson tapped the book.

She propped Donne's *Songs and Sonnets* against the sugar bowl. The time was she would have been incensed by criticism of Clem.

She dug into her lunch. The time was she would have snatched up Curdy's bottle and poured the wine over their smugly smiling faces. The time was . . .

. . . autumn: bleak gray days, gray-stoned pseudo-Gothic buildings, another university. She was twenty years old with a master's, but she didn't feel especially precocious or brilliant.

"Do you really think," asked her doctoral advisor, "that there's anything new to be said about Shakespeare?"

She didn't answer him. She hated him, a hawk-faced man with a fierce black beard who frightened her by asking questions as though they were accusations.

She was staring at *Henry V*. He was talking on the phone, and his normally low voice grew sharp with annoyance. She tried not to hear; he was fighting with his wife. She tried to become invisible; his eyes were boring into her. She stood to go; he waved her back into her seat.

What a wretched and peevish fellow is this King of England, to mope with his fat-brained . . .

The phone slammed down.

. . . to mope with his fat-brained . . .

"Sorry, Leona."

"Van Doren says *Henry V* is imperfect. He calls it a puerile appeal to patriotism. He says . . ."

". . . that politics is substituted for poetry." Stegmann reached out for the book and took her hand instead. He was smiling, and the warmth of his smile promised something

47

she'd been seeking all her life.

He put his other hand to her face, then moved it down her throat and slid it inside her blouse, taking her nipple between his fingers; her nature shifted ever so slightly.

They lay naked on his couch. It had not been enjoyable for her. "I'm so happy," she said.

"You should be sad. *Post coitum omne animal triste.*"

"Clem. Can I call you Clem?" He was slender and human without his pipe and pedestal. He was her teacher and her lover and the friend she'd always wanted, who would let her unburden herself of her life. "Can I talk to you?"

"I was sure you were a virgin," he murmured, toying with her pubic hair.

She crouched down and showed him what she'd learned in Edinburgh.

"Fellatio," he said. "From the Latin *fellatus*, past participle of *fellare*, to suck."

Their meetings were once a week; he would wait for her at his yellow oak desk, collar open, legs crossed, smoking.

"Lock the door, dear." He laid his pipe down on the desk, closed the blinds, and watched his student get undressed.

"Why do you want to watch me?" She performed an awkward striptease, trying to scrunch her body up as small as possible.

"Because I like your style."

When subsequent telephone interruptions came, she wasn't involved with *Henry V*, but with Clem's arms and legs and swelling penis.

He extricated himself and picked up the phone. "What is it, Blanche?" He sat down in his swivel chair. "Invite whomever you want; I told you that this morning." He beckoned to Leona.

She got up from the couch and stood before him.

"No, I don't think John Needham would like Elsie

Bruenig, and I wish you would stop trying to promote affairs among our friends." He ran his hand idly down Leona's body.

"The Sheltons are going on a cruise, I think." He jiggled her breasts up and down.

"Absolutely not Bob Wexler." He motioned Leona to open her legs.

"I'll check the list tonight, Blanche. One of my thesis students is standing here waiting for me."

The thesis was one thing they never discussed, but he was a tireless teacher.

"*Contractus*, drawn together, past participle of *contrahere*."

She accepted his arrogance, his pedantic humor, his aloofness.

"Clem, I love . . ."

He put his finger to her lips.

Unable to speak to him the way she wanted, unable to have an orgasm, floundering with her thesis, she was nonetheless fulfilled. He spoke to her softly, talking about his writing, his aspirations, his wife and children, his past.

"I knew a woman in Tunisia, a very lovely woman, who was married to a rug merchant. I had to court her for several weeks. On the morning after I won her, I crept from her bed at dawn and went out into the market. The stalls were just setting up, and the air was still wet with night. I bought all the flowers they had and took them to her room. I tossed them on her bed, covered her in flowers. When she opened her eyes, she thought she was dreaming."

Leona didn't answer. She was otherwise occupied—analingus, from the Latin *anus*, and *lingere*, to lick.

He sometimes referred to particular women as having been good in bed.

"What makes a woman good in bed, Clem?"

"All the things I've taught you."

"But I'm still not good in bed."

"Why do you say that?"

"Because . . . you know. Don't you care that I don't come?"

"Frankly, no."

That morning, giving Clem his pleasure, she felt something new inside her, a stirring, not exactly pleasant, but odd, definitely interesting.

As she was leaving the office, he asked, "How's the thesis going?"

"Van Doren says . . ."

"Forget Shakespeare."

"Forget Shakespeare?"

"I want you to study Christopher Smart."

She turned to the eighteenth-century lunatic Smart, burying herself night after night in the mad poet's mystical ecstasy. Clem changed their conference day from Wednesday to Monday. "I need a little lubrication to ease into the week."

Then he told her to come to him on Fridays too. "To buoy me up for the weekend."

And then he reinstated their Wednesday sessions as well. Her weeks seemed an endless round from her room to the library to Clem's couch, with his penis moving slowly in and out, and the strange new sensations building within her.

"Have you ever been stoned, Leona?"

She shook her head, watching him as he filled his pipe with a crumbly claylike substance.

"You don't know how to inhale either, do you. . . . It's like sucking in air, very gently. Now hold your breath."

She held her breath until spots appeared before her eyes.

"Enough. You're not supposed to pass out. Here, dear, again."

She smoked the whole bowlful. "I'm not stoned."

"Don't worry about it."

"Really, Clem, I'm not stoned at all." She felt herself grinning stupidly and thinking how funny it was to be sitting naked with her thesis advisor, nice really. She giggled, ticklish. He wasn't so scary, tickling her. No, he wasn't tickling her, he was only touching her, but his skin, she loved him so much.

There it was again.

Slowly in and out. Slowly in and out. Slowly in and out. Oh, she hated it, hated it. It was a hill, a terrible hill, which he made her climb and climb, on and on, on and on. "Don't stop, Clem, please don't stop." Terrible. Worse and worse. In and out. The bells. His ten o'clock class.

"Don't worry, Leona, I'm not going to leave you."

On and on, on and on, and she'd never get to the top, never, never, never, never. "Oh, Clem, Clem, Clem!"

She lay on her side, exhausted, amazed, triumphant.

"Don't cry, dear."

"Oh, Clem." She hugged him as tight as she could.

"You're choking me."

"Can I stay with you today? I'll be quiet. I won't bother you."

"I'm swamped with work." He was putting on his clothes, and his tone of voice meant she should leave him alone now.

At the door, she turned, remembering the bells. He'd skipped his class so she could get over the hill.

He looked up and gave her the V-for-victory sign.

For a short while, they had conferences four times a week.

"Who would have thought when you first appeared in my office, looking like the last lonely whooping crane, that such delightful things were in store." He freed himself from her leggy embrace. "I'm glad it's gotten good for you, Leona."

"It's molten gold."

"A peculiar metaphor."

She couldn't explain herself and stopped trying, but her orgasms made her feel more normal, less like an accident of nature. They made Clem's remoteness less hurtful. And they bound her to him in gratitude.

He arranged for her to teach a course when he went abroad each summer.

Dear Leona—It's rained all week, both children have flu, and oddly, I think of you. It would be fun to stow you away and pull you out whenever I wanted.

Dear Leona—Venice more foul every year. Only a masochist could enjoy making love in these damn gondolas.

His postcards were unsigned. For the first couple of summers she saved them.

Dear L—Athens again. Blanche insists it was my idea. The heat! I'd like my long drink of water.

Dear L—Perhaps next year I'll get them to go without me. Saw a stunning African girl with designs carved in her face.

Dear L—Blanche sick. I had a ludicrous affair on the boat with a Finn. Remind me to tell you.

As time went on, the growing package of cards appeared foolishly sentimental, the kind of thing Clem would smile at, and she reluctantly threw them away.

L—Paris. Quel change. Nobody's named Monique any more and they've discarded those dangerously pointed brassieres.

L—Charming Dutch girl, dreadfully narcissistic in bed. You've spoiled me completely.

He obtained a lectureship for her.

Once in a while, she saw him walking along the campus, jauntily, his hands in his pockets and some pretty student or another hanging on his words.

"What can I do for you?" she asked hesitantly. "Something no one else would do for you?"

"Do you know, Leona"—she was washing him between

the toes with her tongue—"in Japan, you'd be worth a fortune." He laughed, not unkindly.

On the day of the publication of *The Vision of Christopher Smart*, he said to her as though he were handing her a diploma, buttoning her into her blouse, "I've taught you everything I know."

So she came to the University of Atlantic Canada, where she'd been for the past nine years, the victim of Clem's finest joke—a six-foot-one-inch geisha who knew everything there was to know about an eighteenth-century madman whom no one wanted to read.

The chairs at the next table scraped; Wilson and Curdy got to their feet.

"Here you are, Leona." The book was tossed onto her table, knocking over Donne.

She turned the book around and looked at the photograph. His hair was longer, his beard grayer, the lines on his face more numerous. Otherwise, he barely changed from book jacket to book jacket.

In the first shock of being without him, in the first numb months on the strange campus, she'd tried to stoke the fires of the past by remembering things. Their five years became the five beads of her rosary, and their positions on his couch became her litany, which she told and retold, until she forgot.

The forgetting was as much of a shock as their parting, for unlike the parting, it was something she'd never expected. Gradually, she realized—when it was too late—she should have stayed with him, even if it meant accepting nothing more than the crumbs of his days. Anything was better than this absence of all feeling.

She got up, glancing again at the photograph. If he hadn't changed much, neither had she.

She'd grown older. She'd traded her dungarees for tweeds, her sneakers for oxfords, and some of her gaucheness had hardened into mannishness. She'd learned to carry on a conversation like the rest of them, defending herself with barbs and cleverness. But all of that was superficial; when the chips were down, she was what she'd always been, a timid clumsy freak.

She left the cafeteria and walked out into the bright sun, carrying Clem's latest book.

If he returned, he'd say, "Hello, Leona. Still shuffling your feet, I see."

She'd nod her head.

"We had some good times, didn't we."

She'd nod her head.

"Have you found someone else? No one? What have you done all these years?"

She'd smile at him, a mute giraffe.

"Who else would have been so faithful?" He'd laugh, not unkindly, reaching out for the book, and taking her hand instead.

They watched TV during supper. There was a good show on, about a hyena who kills a wildebeest and sucks out the guts.

"I feel sorry for the wildebeest," sniveled Janie.

"Eat your beans."

"It's just nature," explained Bliss.

The wildebeest took a look time dying, and you could hear it howling all the while the hyena ripped it open.

"If you grew up the way we did," said Hazel to her daughter, "you'd think nothing of it. We killed all our meat."

Janie made a face and spat her sausage back in the bowl.

"Here you!" Hazel cuffed her.

"I hate this show."

"Ain't it supposed to be for kids?" Bliss put down his bowl and picked up the *TV Guide*. "There you are. Educational."

"She'd like it more-so in color."

"No I wouldn't."

Hazel cuffed her again, on her way to the sink with the dishes.

Bliss took up the dish towel. "You can switch to something you like now, Janie."

Hazel sloshed the dishes in soapy water and put them on the drainboard. "I was over to Stella's today, watching Young Tony Andrews in color."

"Joey do anything today?"

"He pulled Stella's earring off."

"Likes anything that shines, don't he." Bliss dried a bowl. "Just like a crow."

"Ain't nothing on," said Janie.

"Time for your bed anyways," said Hazel.

"It's still light out!"

"But it's late, and you got school tomorrow."

"Go ahead," said Bliss. "You don't want to fall asleep in school."

"Did you used to fall asleep in school, Daddy?"

"Sometimes."

"Them days was different," said Hazel. "Your father worked in the woods besides going to school."

"Tell me about it, Daddy."

"She's playing for time."

"Get going," said Bliss. "When you're in bed, I'll tell you."

Janie disappeared into the other room, where Joey was already asleep in his crib.

"Oh, she's smart all right," said Hazel. "Be a sight

smarter if she had a color TV."

"She sees the same shows as the other kids."

"Day comes she's the only one don't know a pig is pink nor an elephant's gray, she'll look mighty dumb now, won't she."

"I'm ready, Daddy!"

"Get it over with," said Hazel.

Bliss went into the children's room, where Janie was snuggling under the covers.

"What about when you worked in the woods and fell asleep in school?"

"I took my sled out in the morning, see, with grub for the men, and out again in the evening."

"And who pulled the sled?"

"My dog."

"What was his name?"

"Woolly."

"What did he look like?"

"Woolly, like a lamb."

"What color?"

"Kind of a dirty white."

"And what could he do?"

"Roll over and catch rats and pull the sled."

"What happened to him?"

"A bear got him."

"And did you cry?"

Hazel stood in the doorway with her hands on her hips. "She heard them stories a hundred times."

"Go to sleep now." Bliss gave Janie a kiss, and they shut the door behind them.

"Did you have a good day, hon?"

"Not too bad." Hazel led him back in front of the TV.

"I'm going to open the bed, okay?"

"Go ahead." She switched the channel.

Bliss made up the couch they slept on. "Why don't we watch the TV from over here?"

She sat down beside him; he kissed her throat.

"Stella's set come from Easy Credit Electric."

He cuddled her arms. She didn't mind the feel of him. He was slow and gentle, not like some she could name.

He put one hand over her breast. It felt good, his hand on her breast. It was lovely being a woman with big soft breasts for a man to feel.

He worked his other hand down along her hips. They spread, her hips had, but Bliss didn't mind. More for him to squeeze, he said. She wriggled them a little.

He rolled her sweater up and unhooked her bra, kissing her breasts. She liked when he did that. She could feel it down all through her.

She opened her zipper for him so he could put his hand down her slacks, let him feel her cushiony belly, let him stick his hand inside her panties, let him kiss her on the mouth. It was only the news on.

She put her hand on his trousers. He was hard already. They'd be done in time for the movie.

He took off her clothes for her. She always liked it for a boy to take off her clothes. Tom Flagerty hadn't bothered. He only lifted her skirt and told her to pull down her drawers. In some ways she was better off with Bliss. He riled her right, rubbing her high the way she liked it. Course, with Tom, she might have learned him different. A man learns what a woman likes, same as Bliss learned just what she liked.

He was up, getting undressed himself. She could see they wasn't even to the weather yet. They'd be done for the movie and time to spare. It was that one about Lana Turner and her daughter who killed her sweetheart. Imagine, seeing your man stuck through with a knife, like an animal.

He put his finger in her, feeling to see if she was ready. He must have been handsome, that man of Lana Turner's.

Maybe the daughter fancied him too. You never knew, the sinful life they lived in movies.

For a big man, Bliss wasn't heavy. Some boys put all their weight on top of you. His breath wasn't foul neither. Some boys was so drunk, it made you sick just to kiss them.

She didn't mind kissing Bliss. She even gave him her tongue sometimes for mischief, to see how it stirred him up like. She gave it to him now, sticking her tongue between his lips, twirling it round in his mouth, making him pant like a dog.

He was putting his hands beneath her bum. She was getting heavy for that, but she liked it, Lord, she couldn't deny it, liked his hands beneath her bum, spreading her bum apart.

He offered to have the operation instead of her, but she wouldn't let him. She heard tell it could make a man lose his wants. So she took the pill, and if Dr. Ross changed his mind, she'd have the other. What good would he be if he lost his wants for her?

She wondered how Tom Flagerty did it with his wife. Did he lift her skirt and push her against the wall like he done that time with me in back of the church hall?

Suppose this was Tom Flagerty. Suppose he married me, and he was laying on me now, spreading my bum with his hands and doing them fancy push-ups.

They'd be on a regular bed of course, not this couch-bed. And her gown might be satin, like the one she seen in the catalogue, the one that opened in front, top and bottom, just the ticket for a man like Tom Flagerty, who didn't want to take her clothes off.

He was stopping to wait for her. That was one thing about Bliss, he always waited for her. Would Tom be waiting for her?

She moved her hips up and down, rubbing herself

against him where she liked it, and Tom moved up and down, going a little faster, cause he knew she was almost ready, so he went a little faster, here on their regular bed with the satin sheets and the gown from Sears.

He was lighting a cigarette as she stepped into the sunlight.

"Mr. Dawson?"

"Afternoon."

"I have some work for you. I mean, if you have the time."

"I got the time." He smiled. "Just finishing up for the day."

"It's at my house."

"Will I need to bring any tools?"

"There's a toolbox on the shed, but I couldn't tell you what's in it."

"Repair work, eh?" He scratched his head. "I have to call the wife first."

"You can call from my office."

"Is your house handy?"

"About half a mile."

"I can wait till we get there."

"I don't have a telephone."

"No phone?" He stomped behind her up the stairs.

She left him alone in her office and stood in the hallway. Why shouldn't I have him do the job if he needs the money, and the house needs work?

The last work had been done eight years ago by Mr. Fudge, who'd stolen a stone crock. Perhaps he'd taken other things too, but she'd just moved in and wasn't sure of the inventory. She'd seen the crock in the back of his truck as he drove away one evening, waving. She couldn't think of how to mention it, and never did. Then she began to worry that he knew she knew; so she overpaid him. After that, she let things slide rather than call Mr. Fudge again, or another stranger.

Bliss came out of the office, smiling. "Hazel's in a great humor. She loves to see me working."

"You do a lot of work on your own?" They were going down the stairs.

"Not enough for Hazel."

She breathed the soft spring air and the rough tobacco warmth of the man beside her, who was loping up the road in long booted strides.

He followed a narrow driveway which led behind the hothouses to a small lot, and they stopped at a jalopy painted two different colors.

He opened the door for her; she got in beside him, folding up her long legs, tugging her skirt down over her knees.

"It ain't too roomy," he apologized, turning on the

motor, tilting his head to listen. "She sounds all right tonight."

The old car lurched forward and took them out of the lot, down the hill.

"Where do you live?"

"Do you know where Farrier Lane is?"

"In back of Alling Street? I didn't think no one lived in Farrier Lane."

"I'm the only one. I have a cottage there."

When she'd looked for a place within walking distance of the university, she'd discovered there were no apartments, just houses with family rooms, finished basements, master bedrooms, nurseries—vast sprawling houses, where she would ramble alone like a caretaker. She'd boarded for a while at a rooming house which took in students, and sat silent at the greasy suppers, feeling her professorial presence hanging over the table like a pall.

One evening, taking what she'd thought was a shortcut through a little alley behind Alling Street, she'd found her Shakespearean cottage. The roof was steel rather than thatch; the walls were shingled and not whitewashed; but the windows had tiny panes, the size and shape of the house was almost doll-like, and it sat by itself back among the trees in a secretive, fairy-tale way. It was enchanted for sure; how else had it escaped the bulldozer's blades?

She had made inquiries. The owners didn't want to rent any more to college folk—who always needed work done and cleared out without paying at the end of semester—but when offered what they considered a sucker's price, they changed their policy.

"Turn left here."

They bumped down a gravel lane.

"This is it," she said.

The car ground to a halt, and they stepped out onto the grass.

"It does need some repair," he said.

She looked at her enchanted cottage. The doors and windows hung askew. Many of the weathered shingles were missing. The roof was rusted.

The lawn was a tangle of weeds. They walked up the path, through the shed into the house.

"Well," he said, "it's all a person needs, ain't it? Just a place to flop down."

"Don't you think it's light and airy?"

"Yup." He looked at the cockeyed windows.

"No traffic," she said.

"I like a quiet place myself." He walked around the one big room. "What did you have in mind?"

"The roof leaks."

He kicked the half-filled bucket, which stood beneath a stain on the ceiling. "Have any extra tin?"

"I think I've seen some tin."

They looked in the shed. He gathered up tin, a hammer, a can of nails.

They dragged the ladder out to the yard, and she held it as he climbed up.

"You don't need to hold it."

She leaned against the ladder, thinking about her cottage. She'd been remiss in letting it get so run-down. It was fortunate she'd found someone honest to fix it. Oafish but honest.

His hammer rang on the steel.

She looked up. All she could see was the underside of the eaves, but she had a vision of how he looked, crouched on the slanting roof, his massive shoulders tensed, the muscles in his back rippling beneath his dark green shirt.

The shirt came flying down and landed on the grass.

His back would be bare now, bronze. "Are you okay?"

"You'll see me coming down if I ain't."

She left the ladder for a moment, then walked back to it, the green shirt in her hand.

"Needs some 'lumium paint."

"I know," she said, and touched her face with his shirt. It smelled of car grease and nicotine and spruce and spring weather. His own smell was faint, a delicate thread in the fabric.

The ladder shook. His boots were above her head.

"Should be lots quieter without that drip." His skin wasn't bronze, was white, with only a glow of pink from the May sun. He put on his shirt, and hauled the ladder back into the shed.

"There's a lot to be done if a person thought it was worth it." He stood beside her in the room. "A person's probably better off tearing it down and starting over."

"A person wouldn't want to do that."

He took out tobacco and paper. Something about his dirty fingers rolling the cigarette made her ashamed of mimicking him.

"You see, I like the house," she said.

"It puts me in mind of a camp I stayed one year, when I was cutting in the woods." He threw his match on the floor. "It's comfortable-like, ain't it."

She looked at the match on the floor. Should she offer him an ashtray?

"The thing about a shack," he said, "a feller feels easy in it."

"Yes, there's always that about a shack." My Shakespearean shack.

"Got a bathroom?"

She started to show him, then only pointed.

He opened the door and looked. "Bathroom's good anyways." He shut the door. "You wouldn't have a corking gun, would you?"

"I'm not sure I know what a corking gun looks like."

"That new patch on the roof, see, has to be corked."

"There might be one on the shed."

"What about trowels? Place could use a bit of plastering."

"I don't know. I've never really gone through the tools on the shed."

"Mind if I see what all's there?" He stomped back out.

She turned on the hot plate and put on the kettle, listening to him crashing around in the shed, pulling things out, throwing other things about, the sound of a man who knew how to cope with junk.

She measured out the tea. He'd been so white without his shirt, flushed pink like a shrimp, not at all the way she'd expected such a muscular brute to be.

The door slammed. "Whoever had this place before saved everything from a lady's fart to a clap of thunder."

She smiled. "Did you find what you wanted?"

"Nope."

She put two mugs on the table.

"None for me," he said. "I must get home to supper." But he sat down in a rush-seated chair, and rolled another cigarette. "Landlord don't do no repairs, eh?"

"No." She took out a box of cake. "Mr. Fudge did some repairs a few years ago."

"Old Charlie Fudge?"

"Yes."

Bliss shook his head. "I bet he took you."

She poured the tea.

"He's a good feller, mind you, old Charlie is." Bliss forked off a piece of cake. "Just crooked." He laid his cigarette on the edge of the table, and between bites, picked it up, inhaled, coughed, laid it down again. "Shot Hazel's father in the leg one time."

"My God!"

"They was great friends, the pair of them. Charlie took it into his mind that Jack was after his woman, so he thought he'd learn him a lesson."

"Did he kill him?"

"In the leg?" Bliss went into a fit of laughing, coughing on his cigarette. "I guess that's far enough away from a feller's heart so it wouldn't kill him."

"And was he . . . after his woman?"

"Some says one thing. Some says another."

They sipped their tea.

"Do you have a gun?" she asked.

"I got two guns."

"Did you ever shoot a person?"

"Nope." He finished his cake. "I ain't a drinker."

"What do you shoot?"

"Partridge. But mostly, I like to fish." He stood slowly. "It sure puts me in mind of that camp, when I was cutting in the woods that year, back of Micwam Brook."

"How much do I owe you?"

He scratched his head. "Three dollars all right?"

"You've been here for more than an hour." She looked at her watch. "Closer to three."

"But I only fixed the roof."

She gave him six dollars. "Will you have time for the plastering?"

"Whenever it suits you."

"Tomorrow would be all right." She stood at the door. The cool of evening touched the tangle of her lawn, lifting its green fragrance to her nostrils, and the breeze caressed her skin.

"Tomorrow," he answered.

He lumbered to his jalopy, his baggy bulk caught in the rays of the setting sun.

"Thanks," she called.

He nodded without turning, then bent to open the car door.

It started with a cough, like its master, and she could see him tilting his head to listen. The sound of the engine seemed to please him; he backed up the lane, turned left and chugged off up Alling Street.

The ten dollars Mrs. McFee charged for the course would be saved on a single dress. The hundred-forty for the zigzag portable only come to ten more on their Household Finance All-Inclusive. That was twenty dollars total.

She poured milk on Bliss's Sugar Crisps. "Most everyone's signed up, even plenty who can sew already. That shows something, don't it?"

"What does it show?"

"Why would they pay ten good dollars to take lessons when they already know how to sew, unless Mrs. McFee ain't some good teacher."

Bliss spooned his cereal. "Maybe we can find a second-hand machine at Singer's."

"It wouldn't do buttonholes."

"Don't your dresses all have a zipper?"

"Nor it wouldn't have no zipper foot neither. I'd have to go buy a zipper foot to put onto it. That's another two-three dollars right there. Add on the extras, it's a bargain." She plunked the catalogue down next to the bowls. "There it is. Gold Star Value."

Bliss peered down at the page. "What's this eighty-nine-dollar one?"

"Eh?"

"This here one at the bottom of the page."

"Well, it ain't a zigzag, see?" She pulled the catalogue away, and hustled Janie into her dress.

Bliss stood up from the table. "Mom just used an old foot treadle."

"She hauled her water too."

"Everybody did."

"And now everybody has a zigzag."

Bliss picked up the two lunch pails and waited for his daughter. "What about Mabel? Don't she sew good on a treadle?"

Hazel was stumped for a minute.

"Here I am, Daddy."

"See here, Bliss, it's only for the kids. They'll want nice clothes same as the others, not stuff that looks like it was done up on some old treadle. Five or six more years, Janie'll be busing in to Town. She'll want pretty things, won't you, Janie?"

"I will, Daddy. I'll want pantsuits and pretty things same as the others." They went through the shed, out toward the car.

"You just think on it," shouted Hazel.

The car pulled away.

She looked at her watch, ran back into the house, and filled the tub with water.

Land, a bath was a lovely thing. She washed today without dawdling. Usually, she took her time, rubbing herself up and down with her cake of soap, wallowing in the steam and thinking back on them years she heated water on the stove just to get enough to dab here and there with a rag. A bath was lovely, but today she better not dawdle.

She changed and fed the baby, letting him drink his milk while she put on her new red wig, zipped up her jumpsuit, buttoned her blazer, and caught a few minutes of Private Practice.

Stove's out. Curtains closed. Diaper bag packed. She checked the house one more time, then took Joey in her arms, locked the door, and waded through the bushes to Mabel's house.

Mabel's windows were open, and her rugs hung over the sills. Lord love the poor old soul, beating rugs in her condition. Hazel kicked a couple of mangy cats out of her way, and knocked on the door.

She heard Mabel feeling through the house, groping for the knob.

"If it ain't Hazel and Joey!"

"I'm catching the bus in." Hazel handed her the baby and his diaper bag.

Mabel nuzzled Joey with her nose; her eyes were about as good as a groundhog's. "We'll have a nice time, won't we, lambie-pie."

"I'll be back on the three o'clock." Hazel slipped the old woman a dollar; it wasn't much, but Mabel was related, somewheres back in Bliss's family, grandfather's cousins and such.

"No rush, Hazel."

71

"See you later, Mabel."

Hazel cut through the woods to the highway. It sure was a grand day for traveling the roads!

Cars zoomed past, stirring up dust.

She stepped back so as not to dirty her suit or wig.

Far off, she could see the bus approaching, coming fast, now slower.

"Grand day, eh?" She stepped up.

"All the way?"

"Yup."

"A dollar eighty."

She counted out the change, and found herself a seat, settling in with her pocketbook, the one she usually saved for funerals.

Out the window, the last of Fingabog Siding was past. There was Patterson's farm, cows and pigs mucking about in the mud. There was Moffat's Parts, a bunch of rusted cars. Price's Hill. The weighing station. Laughlin's Esso.

She took the mirror out of her handbag and straightened her wig. It was real natural, not like them cheap ones. Eterna-Curl. The way the saleslady explained it, it was like wash 'n' wear, but more-so.

There was Temperance Hollow, smaller than Fingabog Siding, not even no post office. A few old houses. Trailers.

Trailers was cute inside. Each piece new and in its place. Her sister Min used to live in a trailer, with brown and orange curtains, everything a woman would want. And then she left it all for some nigger. Left a husband who waxed floors in the hospital, two little children, a practically brand-new trailer. There was no understanding some people.

They moved to Chicago, but they visited once, Min and her nigger. Janie'd been a baby then in the cradle. The nigger sat on the steps smoking tailor-made cigarettes, and Min said she liked it out to Chicago.

There was Pedico Village, with a mill and a high school

of its own and a bowling alley. She could see the smoke from the mill. Brick houses them people lived in, supposed to be three bricks deep. She wouldn't care for one—dirty old red brick.

There was O'Haras' house by the tracks. Welfare built it for them. Imagine that. People that didn't work did better than them that did. Here was her and Bliss working every day at the college and odd jobs too, and O'Haras living just as good from the government. She wouldn't be surprised if they had a color TV.

Now that was a pretty house, with its windows on a slant-like. It was getting to be all the rage, them slanty picture windows.

Coming closer, Shannon Road, with its falling-down shacks, a dozen kids in each and half as many dogs. It was a scandal, them tarpaper shacks, most of the folks not even married. Still, it was awful close to Town. A person could fix up one of them shacks.

They rumbled over the bridge, and Hazel checked her mirror again. She patted her wig and tested her smile.

The bus was rolling down Front Street—the bank, dress shops, movie house, the bus terminal.

She shouldered her purse, stepping down to the sidewalk.

Hustle and bustle!

She made her way to the corner, squared her shoulders and walked into Abernathy Realty.

"Good morning."

"Morning."

"May I help you?"

"I wanted to look at a house."

"Just one moment. Mr. Johnstone, can you speak to this lady?"

"Good morning . . . Beautiful day . . . Won't you come into my office?"

Hazel followed the checkered suit, tiny little checkers, with two flaps and cuffs and shiny shoes.

"What exactly was it you were looking for?"

She smiled back at him, flashing her dimples, and took the seat he pulled out for her. "That new house across from the K-Mart."

"That's a three-bedroom, two stories. Is that what you had in mind?"

"Yes."

"It's fifty thousand."

"That's about what I figured on paying."

"Well now, Mrs. . . . ?"

"Mrs. Smith."

"Well now, Mrs. Smith, we have several other homes in that price range."

"I just wanted to look at that one."

"I see." He stood up. "Bruce, do you have the keys to the two-story across from the K-Mart?"

A younger man came into the office. He smiled at Hazel, and she dimpled back.

"That's an excellent buy," he said. "A fully finished basement, two fireplaces, family room."

"Cheap for all that, isn't it?"

"Yes it is, Mrs. Smith." Mr. Johnstone was leading her out into the glory of Front Street. "My car is right around here. We have our own parking lot; saves so much time looking for a space."

"I know we have an awful time getting a parking spot," she agreed.

"Do you live in town, Mrs. Smith?"

"No, but we come in quite a bit."

"I see, you live out of town?"

"North."

"Nice country up north."

"We want to be handier." She was stepping into his car,

leather seats and a head rest and a lovely dash with a custom radio and seat belts. "My husband works here in town."

"Where does he work?"

"In an office."

"I see."

"He does book work in an office."

"Well, it would be handier." He was driving them through town, just a-cruising over Front Street, in a custard-color car with leather seats and her jumpsuit and her new red wig and a man in a checkered suit.

They were passing the bank. Tom Flagerty might look out. She rolled down the window to get the air.

"It is a warm day for May," said Mr. Johnstone.

They passed the bank. She rolled the window up; no point in messing her wig for nothing.

"Have any children, Mrs. Smith?"

"Two."

"Just the right size house for you."

"I like them fairy bricks on the front."

"They're very popular, fairy bricks. They're not exactly bricks. They come in a sheet."

"More like plywood."

"That's right. They come in sheets like plywood."

The custard car was climbing the K-Mart hill, past the lawns with their tulips and daffodils and figurines.

"Nice neighborhood," said Hazel.

"The people take pride in their homes."

"That's what I like."

"Is your present home, up north, an older home?"

"Oh no, it's quite new."

"Perhaps we can sell it for you."

"There's quite a few wouldn't mind having it."

"Here we are," he said.

There it was, smack across from the K, fairy brick, picture window, the stickers still on the glass, white steps with curly railings, which Hazel held on to, following Mr. Johnstone up into the foyer.

Well!

"An unusual touch," said Mr. Johnstone.

She never seen the like of it—papered clear across the foyer wall, men and ladies in their nightgowns going crazy.

"A Roman pastorale."

"I don't know," said Hazel. "I'm Pentecostal."

"I don't know myself," said Mr. Johnstone. "Ancient art. Some people like it."

"What do you call it?"

"A pastorale."

It had a sort of a sound to it. *Won't you come in for a cup of tea? Leave your boots on the mat, under my pastorale.*

"The contractors might replace it."

"No," said Hazel. "I think it suits me."

"Now this is the living room."

She went straight for the picture window. There it was, the K. Everyone went there sooner or later. She struck a natural pose. Wouldn't I be a picture, standing in my window. "Course, it needs drapes."

"Drapes make all the difference."

"They don't open, do they."

"You open the other windows. Plenty of windows, all aluminum, Thermopane, guaranteed for ten years."

She strutted over to the fireplace, and leaned her arm on the mantle. Up above the wall, she'd hang two big pictures, one her, one Bliss, like in the magazines. Autographed originals.

"There's another fireplace in the family room."

Why was he rushing her? She circled the living room, peering down at the baseboard. "Plenty of plugs."

"The house is completely electric."

"I thought I'd get an electric organ."

"We're thinking of getting one ourselves." He was lead-

ing her out of the living room into . . . look at the chandelier, would you!

"Your dining room."

It was all candles and gold and glass like drops of water,
glittering like diamonds. "Would you mind turning it on?"

Imagine eating under that! How could you watch TV
with that there blaze of light?

"Let me see," said Mr. Johnstone. "Here we are."

"It's going out."

"That's the dimmer switch."

So that's how you watched the TV. "May I try that?"
She put her hand to the switch, and made the candles grow
bright, then turned them down.

"Here's your kitchen."

She followed him through the doorway. Enough cupboards for an army.

"Here's your range. Wall oven. Fridge. Dishwasher.
Garbage-eater. Revolving corner cupboards."

Hazel was getting dizzy. It would take her all day just to
look at the kitchen, opening and shutting doors, pressing
buttons, figuring out how to run it.

"Self-defrosting, continuous-clean, everything guaranteed."

She opened the fridge door, as white as white, with bins
and crispers and dairy partitions.

"The family room's downstairs."

How could she see everything when he went so fast? She
hurried down after him. Mr. Johnstone wasn't much of a
salesman.

"Your family room."

All knotty-pine panels with the fireplace and a bar. "I'm
Pentecostal," she repeated automatically.

"You can just use it for a serving bar. Or, some people
I've seen convert them into soda fountains."

Now that! She was crazy for ice cream. So was Janie and

so was Bliss. And soda. And ices. *Would you like a sundae or a banana split?* "How much would that cost?"

"I don't know," he said. "I don't imagine more than a thousand."

"Well worth it."

He was dragging her out. "Your laundry room."

A washer and a dryer and a great big sink and a little sink and a flush. "Ain't there no bathtub?"

"Your baths are upstairs."

Up they went again, and up some more.

"This is the master bedroom."

This is where they'd sleep, her and Bliss, in a bed with a canopy onto it. She seen one on TV, ruffles all around it. Terrible for catching dust; still, they was probably wash 'n' wear. She patted her wig.

"Wall-to-wall closets."

Lord, she could buy every dress in the K-Mart, and pantsuits and jumpsuits and negligees.

"Master bathroom."

"Another one of them do-hicks."

"Pastorale."

Leaping in their nighties over her while she bathed. Be embarrassing. Course, it was only a picture. Glass doors to make it more private.

"Through here . . ."

He didn't give her time to see nothing. For fifty thousand dollars, you'd think he'd let her dawdle.

"The larger of the two other bedrooms."

This one would be for Joey. A view of the K-Mart and all. Too bad the master bedroom didn't look on the front.

"And the smaller."

Nice for Janie. They could paper it with animals.

"The children's bath."

Who was going to clean all them bathrooms? At least it didn't have no Romans prancing about.

"The attic is strictly for storage." He opened a door in the ceiling, pulling down a folding ladder, and closed it up again. She would have liked to go up and snoop around, but what could you do? He was going back downstairs.

"What do you think?"

"Course"—she followed him out of the house—"I'll have to let my husband take a look."

"I wouldn't wait too long." Mr. Johnstone opened the door of his car. "It's a very choice location."

"I think I'll stick around." She didn't get into the car. "Look at the yard and such."

"Hope you don't mind me rushing off. I have several other appointments."

"Not a bit."

"Here's my card."

She watched the custard car drive off, then crossed the highway and walked through the Plaza into the K-Mart.

On a sudden impulse, she decided to pass the two students who'd been expecting failure. Several times she'd gotten up from figuring grades, and looked out the window at the sunny day.

Once he'd been bent over his shovel, his skin gleaming like milk. Another time he'd been smoking with the other man, the two of them coughing comfortably together. She'd seen him sitting on the grass, eating a sandwich from his lunch pail, and afterward lying back, his arms above his head, armpits tufted brown.

Occasionally the two men talked, and she put her pen down and listened to their voices drifting in through the open window.

"I put my peas in last night."

"Good weather for putting in peas."

And then their shovels sounded again.

"I seen the fiddleheads are up."

"Would they be in the stores yet?"

At two o'clock, they disappeared behind the building, and she walked downstairs, continuing on into town—the weather was so fine—and bought a pound of fiddlehead ferns.

Now it was four-fifteen.

She turned away from the desk and leaned back in her chair, crossing her feet on the low metal cabinet.

Herring boxes without topses, sang the children, *sandals were for Lee-o-na.*

She'd tried to play basketball. Everyone thought she'd be good at that, but she wasn't. She was uncoordinated, timid of the ball and of the other children darting about her.

She'd been poor at all the sports except for swimming, where with her body hidden in an alien element, she found a secret grace.

"I guess it's time," said the older man, "to see what the neighbors are having for dinner."

"See you tomorrow," said Bliss.

Leona swung her feet to the tile, collected her bag, her briefcase, the fiddleheads.

She stepped outside.

He looked up from the cigarette he was rolling and smiled.

They loped up the road together, and followed the path behind the hothouses; the blue and rust jalopy waited in the lot.

For a moment it sounded as if it wouldn't start, but he turned the key again gently, pressing his foot down just the right amount, listening to its needs with his head slightly cocked; it couldn't resist.

They drove down the hill.

"Term's pretty well done for you, I guess."

"I teach summer school."

"Don't care for traveling, eh?"

"Oh, you know, those dreary Grecian ruins and *filet cheval*." She immediately saw that he didn't know. "Traveling makes me lonely." Yes, that was the truth. At home, among her books and a routine, she could lose herself. In foreign countries, surrounded by strangers, she felt like a monolith.

"I went down to New Hampshire once." He steered left on Sussex. "They got a mountain there looks just like a person."

"Were you on vacation?"

"Trucking." He turned left on Alling. "There's a machine, see, you put ten cents in, and then you can look at the mountain real good."

They pulled up in front of her house.

He opened the trunk of the car and took out some tools, a tube, a sack of something.

"I'll cork that roof first."

She helped him out with the ladder. He climbed up with his caulking gun, and she watched him disappear, shoulders, shirt, pants, and finally boots.

She found herself clutching the wooden rungs. What was she being so desperate about? Was she afraid he'd fall down and sue her?

She forced herself away from the ladder.

He was very conscientious, remembering to bring everything. But then, why shouldn't he be? He wasn't an idiot, just a bumpkin. A soft-spoken, thoughtful bumpkin.

"That's done," he said, rolling a cigarette. She stood beside him in the warmth of the sun, tasting his smoke in her nose.

There were worse ways to spend an evening than standing around watching the world from a weedy dooryard. She'd seen an old couple once from the window of a train, sitting on a farm porch, staring into space, and she'd laughed.

"Old Man Mountain," she said.

"You seen it too?"

"And I put a dime in the machine." Never but never would she admit doing such a corny thing to anyone who mattered.

He finished his cigarette. "I guess I'll patch them walls."

They put the ladder away.

"Mind if I use the drip bucket? You don't need it no more." He poured some powder from his sack into the bucket, added water, and stirred it to a gray paste, moving his stick through the thick mixture. With the first trowel, he dabbed the paste over a crack, and with the second trowel, he planed it smooth.

She opened her briefcase, and took out the last class's exams.

He covered the jagged chinks around the windows, the cracks in the corners, the gashes where the house had settled, healing wound after wound.

"May I try it?"

He handed the trowels over.

She glopped on too much, scraped it off, made a mess.

"You ain't patient enough."

She gave him back his tools.

"I know where I can borrow another set of trowels," he said, returning to his work, "if you want to try your hand. Only you got to go at it more gentle-like."

She put the water on for the fiddleheads and cleaned them carefully, trying to go at it with patience, unfurling each little spiral, washing off the brown bits of winter coat which still clung to the fronds.

When the greens were boiling, she set the table, putting

83

her favorite plate, a blue and white antique, at the place where he'd sat yesterday.

His trowels clattered in the bucket. "That's the batch." He followed his nose to the pot. "Ain't they lovely? Nice young clean ones." He twitched his nose like a rabbit. "They're ready."

She ladled them out with a slotted scoop.

"We used to pick them down at the Micwam Brook," he said between forkfuls. "They come up there before they come up anywheres else. As soon as the floods went down, there they was along the bank, growing in amongst the moss and cedar."

She could see him—pre-oaf days, a round-headed child, in amongst the moss and cedar.

"Ain't you eating yours?"

She took a bite and chewed it.

He shoveled the ferns into his mouth in buttery clusters, lips shining. "After we picked them all, we sold them. Twenty-five cents a bag. Most everyone would want some, them being the first of the year."

She imagined him walking from house to house, his thick body young and delicate, in overalls, barefoot. It was probably just the opposite. He probably set up a stand by the side of the road and fleeced the tourists.

"Did you have a stand?"

"Nope. We went from house to house."

"Were you barefoot?"

"We wore shoe-pacs."

"What are shoe-pacs?"

"Well, they're . . ." He scratched his head.

". . . shoe-pacs," she supplied.

"More or less."

She laughed, refilling his empty plate.

"I'm a fine guest I am, eating all your fiddleheads."

"I've had enough."

He nodded his shaggy head. "Some people can't take too much. Janie now, one feed's enough for her. I can eat a dozen platefuls, and it won't hurt me none."

He smiled, spearing the last of them. "Funny how the first of the year is always the best. Just like them ones from the Micwam." He took out his tobacco and rolled a cigarette between his plaster-covered fingers. "I guess a person couldn't get back to the Micwam if they tried now. Roads all growed over."

He leaned both elbows on the table, watching the smoke curl from his cigarette.

A droplet of butter had hardened on his chin.

She put out her hand to wipe it off but thought better of it.

He coughed, continuing his smoky contemplation, then pushed back his chair. "I guess I better."

She got up and went for her purse. "What do I owe you, Mr. Dawson?"

He figured his hours on his napkin. "Pay me once a week if it's easier for you. The old woman don't spend it till Saturday anyways."

When Hazel hung her wash from the special window Bliss built in the shed to save her from going out, she could see June Setzer's wash and her woodpile and her dog, Fats, who was tied up by a chain.

Avery Setzer, June's husband, had caught the mumps too late in life, which is why people said the baby weren't his. Hazel wasn't one to cast the first stone at such a close neighbor. Like Bliss said, *It ain't our lookout.* Besides which, Hazel liked June, a girl with common sense.

Old Mrs. Setzer was stopping for vacation, so Hazel took Joey over when she called for June to go to the sewing class. Mrs. Setzer could watch two babies easy as one.

"Won't you have some tea first, Hazel?" June already

seen the wig, so she didn't have to comment.

"Just a drop," said Hazel.

The story hummed in the background while June poured.

Old Mrs. Setzer was cutting up used tea bags and drying the leaves on the stove.

"Peanut butter cookies!" said Hazel.

"I made them with the crunchy to be different," said June.

Hazel didn't bake cookies herself, just donuts, brown bread, and cake when she had the mind to. "Tasty, ain't they."

"Are you getting the zigzag?"

"Yes," said Hazel. "What about you?"

"Avery's going to get me a second-hand from Singer."

"I suppose them second-hands are just as good."

"He says if the sewing works out, we can always trade up."

"That's a thought, too." Hazel didn't like to brag. "Now that Bliss is working steady evenings, we figured there'd be no point in getting a cheap machine."

"I noticed him coming home late these last few weeks."

"Yes." Hazel sipped her tea. "He's remodeling Miss deVos's house."

"Miss deVos from up the college?"

"Miss Leona deVos."

"I seen her picture in the *Courier*."

"Bliss took on the job."

"Remodeling it for her, is he?"

"It's an older home."

"One of them big old mansions up on College Hill?"

"Handy to College Hill."

"I always wondered what they was like inside."

Hazel broke off a piece of cookie. "She's got a Roman pastorale."

"A what?"

"A pastorale. She got one in the foyer over the boots and a small one over her tub."

"What does it look like?" asked June, forgetting to refill Hazel's cup.

"I'll have a bit more just to hotten it."

June poured.

"It's something like wallpaper," said Hazel, "only it's got people onto it." It didn't sound like much. "You know the Sun Luck Garden? Well, it's more like what they got in the back there where they throw them banquets."

"Over her tub?"

"Yes." Hazel studied her friend's face; June wasn't one for getting too worked up. "And she's got a soda fountain."

"Sounds *exactly* like the Sun Luck Garden!"

Hazel leaned back, satisfied.

"What else does she have?"

"A chandelier with a dimmer switch for watching TV."

"A chandelier for watching TV?"

Hazel skipped it; the pastorale had been hard enough to explain. "And a wall oven and a dishwasher and a garbage-eater."

June shook her head. "Some women have everything."

"And a laundry room."

"Don't sound like it needs much remodeling."

"Oh, you know them old houses. Shingles are bound to fall off. Windows and doors get yee-hawed."

"They don't appear to be yee-hawed from the street."

"Not to you or me, but some women have to have everything perfect."

"That's the truth."

Hazel gazed into her tea. "The lawn's clear covered with tulips."

"She must have a gardener, eh?"

"Naturally Miss deVos don't do her own hoeing."

"I don't blame her," said June. "Specially after the black flies come."

"She's got a woman who comes to clean every day of the week."

"Who would that be, I wonder."

"You wouldn't know her. Some woman from over Mactigouche."

"I suppose she'd get all the clothes."

"I suppose," said Hazel.

"Lord, look at the time!"

Hazel followed her friend into the bedroom.

"I thought I'd wear the red."

"That would be pretty," said Hazel. June had a built-in closet with accordion-pleated doors. "Miss deVos has a wall-to-wall closet."

"Wouldn't I like that!" June took off her muumuu. She was a nice-looking girl, what you'd call petite, not much for a man to grab on to. Course, that wouldn't matter to some men, for example, Tom Flagerty.

"Zip me up, Hazel."

Hazel pulled the zipper. They said the father of June's baby was Gordy Colpitts from down Dribley, feller that come to read the meters. The difference was that Hazel's meter was outside, whereas June's meter was in the kitchen.

June took down her rollers; she did have lovely hair, natural curly. The roots was showing.

"I bought my pattern, did you?"

"Yes." Hazel patted her bag.

They walked back through the kitchen.

"Going now?" Mrs. Setzer was rolling her tea leaves in cigarette paper.

"See you later."

The old lady nodded, and lit up a smoke.

Hazel followed June out of the house. It wasn't but a holler away to the church hall, quite a few cars already parked in front. She pushed open the door.

"Who's that with June Setzer?"

"It's Hazel Dawson!"

"Can't be Hazel!"

"It's me all right." Hazel laughed, touching her wig.

"Puts you in mind of that red-headed actress, you know the one."

"I know who you mean."

"The one that's carrying on with Young Tony Andrews."

"Not Emmeline!" said Hazel. She never would have thought. She must tell Bliss.

"Where'd you get it?"

"Woolworth's."

"Don't it itch?" asked Mrs. McFee.

"Not a bit."

"Is it hot?"

"Course not. It breathes."

"It breathes?"

"All the new ones breathe."

The door opened again, and three more women entered.

"Is that Hazel Dawson?"

"No, it's Emmeline from the TV!" Hazel laughed fit to burst.

"I bet she'd like to carry on with Young Tony Andrews, wouldn't you, Hazel?"

"I ain't answering."

"She does look like Emmeline though, don't she? The dimples and all."

"We can begin now," said Mrs. McFee. She was an awful old poke.

She stood in the hall outside her office, while Bliss phoned home.

"Sorry to keep you waiting."

"That's okay."

"Wasn't no need for you to stand in the hall. There's fifteen with their ear to the telephone out in Fingabog Siding anyways."

She followed his clatter down the stairs. Although summer session hadn't begun, she came to school each day to work on her Donne book, which wasn't going well.

It was amazing how heavily he moved in his boots. He had to be the one person clumsier than she was.

No, she was the clumsiest.

"I'll get it." He stooped to retrieve the books and papers that rolled out of her briefcase.

"I guess the handle snapped."

"No wonder." He put it under his arm. "It ain't supposed to hold a jeezly library."

She tramped up the road beside him. She wished she had the briefcase back. It looked incongruous with his work clothes, his bulk . . . his hands . . . his face . . . with everything about him. They walked the path to the lot behind the hothouses, and got into the Bluebird: that's what she'd named his jalopy while doodling on Donne.

The Bluebird lurched forward.

"I met old Charlie Fudge in town today." They drove down the hill and out through the gates. "Told him I was fixing up Miss deVos's shack."

He honked his horn at a grosbeak sitting in the road. "I told him you was going to be a first-rate plasterer."

They parked in Farrier Lane. He opened the trunk of his car and took out a roll of green wire screening. "It come to me I ought to get something up before the black flies eat you."

"There are screens out in the shed somewhere."

"They been chewed through by mice." He stomped into the shed and showed her.

"Can I help you?"

"Nope."

She deposited her briefcase on the table.

The sun streamed through the windows. It was a beautiful evening, too nice to stay inside.

She opened the door to the shed and saw him blundering among the screens, squinting in the half-light. "It's brighter outside," she suggested.

They carried the screens outside. He knelt in the grass, removing old tacks, taking out the mouse-chewed stuff, fastening new screening to the frames with thin strips of wood.

She sat on the worm-eaten steps, hugging her skirt around herself, her long legs hunched up to her chin.

The green of his shirt matched the green of the screening. The skin on the back of his neck was dark with dirt, streaked white where his sweat had run.

What would her life have been like if she'd been born in the sticks with no ideals or aspirations, just a simple country woman, content to pack her good man's lunch pail and patch his pants and diaper his kids. It didn't sound so terrible. Her good man would be a galumph—well, maybe he'd be a handsome galumph—and she'd be a sweet little thing; but now the whole fantasy fell apart, for it was harder to imagine being a sweet little thing than all the rest of it.

"Miss deVos, will you hold this in place while I fasten it?"

She went to the window and held the screen in place. "Won't you call me Leona?"

"All right, ma'am."

"I know it seems silly, but when people call me by my last name I always think they don't like me. Not that you have to like me to call me Leona, but I feel more as if . . . less as if . . ."

"Makes no odds to me." He screwed the screen on. "My first name's Bliss."

"It's an unusual name, isn't it."

"Not in these parts it ain't. There's Bliss Dumphy and Bliss McBain and Bliss Pond and Bliss Buber. Half a dozen up our way." He went on listing the Blisses while they circled the house, putting up the screens.

"That should keep the buggers out."

"Not the midgies though," she added.

"Nope." He took out tobacco and rolled a cigarette; his fingers were green from the screening. "Nothing will help you against them. You just got to keep the lights out at night." He lit a match. "I was doing book work one time, trying to figure bills and such. Hardly noticed I'd switched on the light, but I got to itching and scratching. Hazel, she come back out from Janie's room and screamed. I was clear black with midgies!" He coughed and shook his head. "Clear black. Hazel run the bath, and I drowned the sons of bitches."

Leona felt a sharp pain beneath her ribs. It was a pain she hadn't experienced in years, not since Clem used to tell her about his wife.

Bliss smoked his cigarette and rubbed his green hands on his shirt, and Leona refused to make the connection.

"That's what comes of staying up late," he concluded.

"Do you go to sleep early?"

"Pretty early. Hazel mostly watches the movies, but it don't bother me. I could fall asleep in the middle of the Sourgrass Fair if I was tired."

She bent down to pick up the bits of scrap left over from the screening.

He bent down beside her. They carried the refuse inside.

"Shall I put up tea?"

"I almost forgot!" He banged out of the shed and over to the Bluebird, rummaged in his lunch pail. "I brought you a donut."

"Did Hazel send it?"

"Nope." He handed her a crumpled ball of wax paper. "I left it over from lunch."

"Thanks."

He looked at the gift and scratched his head. "I thought you might like one."

"I would, a prize-winning donut."

"That's right too," he said. "Second up to Sourgrass."

"Good class today, wasn't it."

"Awful hot in that church hall." Hazel puffed a bit, flapping along the road in her rubber sandals.

"Dust in this weather's terrible."

"Every time a car goes by, it ruins the wash."

"A person really needs a dryer as much in summer as winter."

"More-so. At least in winter, the wash stays clean."

"I imagine I'll be getting one soon."

"That so?" said Hazel.

"I imagine."

"I imagine too."

"You're getting one too, are you?"

"If this dust keeps up, I'll have to."

"That's just it."

"And the way clothespins break nowadays."

"A person can't afford *not* to have a dryer."

They slapped their arms and legs as they walked.

"Black flies seems worse this year."

"I can't put Donny out at all."

"No, I can't put Joey out neither."

They were standing in front of June's house. "Will you come in for some tea?"

"I don't like leaving Joey at Mabel's too long."

Although old Mrs. Setzer was still stopping for vacation, she'd mentioned to June that caring for one baby was enough. June had mentioned it to Hazel. It was a sore point. Not that Hazel didn't like June just as much, but she thought her friend might have explained to Mrs. Setzer how it made it hard on Hazel, taking the baby over to Mabel's, then coming on over to June's, to the church hall, back to Mabel's. Well, she hadn't, and that was that. It was a new highlight on June's character. "No," repeated Hazel. "I better not come in."

"One cup."

"Well, one cup."

"How's the sewing coming?" Mrs. Setzer looked up from Camilla Starr.

"We're up to zippers," said June.

Hazel didn't answer. If Mrs. Setzer couldn't be bothered to keep one eye on Joey, Hazel couldn't be bothered to tell her about the zippers.

"I always sewed mine in by hand," said Mrs. Setzer.

"What happened to Camilla Starr!"

All eyes swerved to the TV set. Camilla's eye was black and blue.

"It's that Miles done it," said Mrs. Setzer.

"Did you see him do it?" asked Hazel, forgetting her grudge.

"He done it last night."

That was something anyways. If they'd been in class while Camilla was getting punched, Hazel would have wondered if sewing was worth it.

"Why does she put up with him?" asked June.

"Love," said old Mrs. Setzer.

"Do you like these gingersnaps?" asked June, over tea.

"Very nice," said Hazel.

"They burnt a little."

"Not so you'd notice."

"I seen Janie go by," said Mrs. Setzer, "carrying a berry basket."

"I told her she could pick berries after school."

"Just letting you know."

"Much obliged," said Hazel. Did that old biddy think she couldn't watch over her own children?

"The midgets are wrestling tonight on TV," said June.

"They're awful cute, ain't they, on them short little legs."

"Take quite a beating though."

"Might not hurt so much, them being so close to the ground."

"Indians going to be on too," said Mrs. Setzer.

"Wasn't that terrible, the other week, when the Monster tore all their feathers out?"

"He ought to be banned, really."

"Did you see him the time he rim-racked the Singing Swinger's guitar?"

"I guess I did! He stomped it to splinters."

"Local boy," said Mrs. Setzer.

"The Singing Swinger?"

"The Monster. His mother come from Upper Waska."

"No!"

"Raised turnips."

"The Monster?"

"Lovely turnips."

"More tea?"

"I can't." Hazel stood. "I don't like to leave Joey too long . . . even though Mabel considers it a treat to have him."

She threw that last bit at Mrs. Setzer.

I come to pluck your berries harsh and crude. She popped one in her mouth; the warm juice spurted down her throat. She'd taken off the afternoon to go to Tupper's U-Pick. She thought her handyman might like some strawberries for tea.

She crawled on her hands and knees, choosing the plumpest, reddest berries, ignoring the flies that swarmed around her.

The walls of the shack were plastered, sanded and painted, and he had said he was going to make shelves for her books, which were piled all over, beside the cot, on chairs, in random heaps on the floor.

She got to her feet, straightening out her stiff limbs. The

blood rushed to her head, and she noticed how hot the sun was.

The road back to town was long. Whenever a car drove past, it left a cloud of dust behind it, which settled on her and her basket. She walked quickly, anxious to get home and wash the fruit, and change back into a dress.

She stopped at Pym's Dairy on Alling Street.

"A pint of heavy cream, please."

"You got quite a burn, Miss deVos."

"I was picking berries." Of course she never tanned, only reddened, then blistered, then peeled.

"Some nasty bites too."

Now she felt the itching.

"Try calamine," called Pym.

She turned into the lane with her packages. The Bluebird was waiting there, its master sitting on the doorstep.

"I took off early." He stopped and stared at her. "You're going to pain some tonight."

"Were you waiting long?" She fumbled for her keys, not knowing which distressed her more, his having waited for her or seeing her like this, covered with dust in a pair of men's overalls.

"Do you have calamine?"

"I'll be okay," she said.

"It'll hurt a lot less if you put some on right away." He picked among the pine boards on the shed. "But suit yourself."

She went inside and washed her face and combed her hair.

There was a bottle of calamine in the cupboard.

She looked in the mirror. She was red as a lobster, swollen with bites, hideous. And she'd look a lot worse if she put lotion on.

She dabbed it on. It was like a mask. One Halloween, when she was about ten, she'd bought a princess mask with a crown. At the last minute, she couldn't live up to it and put on her hobo mask instead.

The lotion was pinky-white. Only her eyes and lips shone out. It was too horrible. She had to wash it off before he returned.

The shed door opened, and he pushed through with the boards, nodding approval at her calamine face.

She laughed. It was ridiculous how she suffered over her looks, when he was so oblivious. He might have been approving the length of a pine board.

"What's so funny?"

"Me. I look like a clown with my white face and baggy pants."

He looked thoughtfully at her overalls. "Good job you was wearing them, or your legs would've got bit too."

"Yes, it is a good job." She felt a sudden rush of freedom. He didn't give a damn what she looked like.

She dumped the berries into a collander, and ran the water through them. He didn't weigh her and find her wanting.

She sifted the berries through her fingers. He accepted her without question—just as he accepted her shack and her crazy books.

She dried the berries gently with a paper towel. Just as he accepted his own lack of education and missing teeth.

Did he even know that he was handsome?

She plucked off the green leaves. He didn't know it. She was sure of it. Maybe he knew that he was strong, knew his eyes were blue, but he wouldn't put it together and set a judgment on it.

Just as he didn't judge her. How splendid the berries were in their ripeness.

"What if I put a shelf over the bed here, so you can grab a book in the evening?"

"That would be fine."

He pushed the cot away from the wall and ran his knuckles along the plaster, testing for the sound of studs.

She carried the berry leaves outside and threw them on the grass, then sat beneath a maple tree, leaning her back against its rough trunk.

The hot sun and picking had tired her, and she dozed off, into dreams of a fantastic garden, filled with shade trees and strawberry plants; she knew from the feeling of grace which fell over her in its bowers that it was the garden of innocence, the unremembered state before she found out she was homely.

When she woke up, her face was stiff in its calamine mask. She shambled back into the shack.

All the shelves were up, and he was ranking them with books, looking at each title to make sure they were standing upright.

She set out the bowls and cream.

"Tea time, eh?" He went out to his car, and came back with the donuts.

She put the kettle on.

"You ought to take the sun more gradual."

"Yes, I should."

They settled into their chairs.

"You picked these at Tupper's, did you?"

She nodded.

"There ain't nothing like berries when the sun's still into them."

"Do you ever pick berries?"

"We used to pick wild ones in home. Janie still picks some." He crushed them with his spoon, stirring cream through the mash. "Berries, fiddleheads, mayflowers, violets, all them things we used to sell."

"I've never seen a mayflower."

"Never?" He looked up from his berries. "Dad always

picked a bunch for Mom every Mother's Day. After he died, I picked them for her. Now I pick them for Hazel."

The pain beneath her ribs was back, a familiar friend. "She must like that."

"Hazel favors plastic." He lifted the bowl to his lips and drank the cream.

Leona brought the rest of the berries to the table. "I always wanted to live in a cottage surrounded by flowers."

"You could plant some around this place."

"I put in bulbs when I first moved here, but they didn't come up."

"Weeds is too thick."

"I guess that's it."

"I ain't much of a gardener."

"I didn't expect you to garden."

"I could. But there's so much other work. What good will flowers do you if your house falls in?"

She smiled. "It's not that bad."

"The shed's quite bad. I'd like to put a jack out there. Jacks run about thirteen dollars."

"That doesn't seem like too much."

"The end should be jilpoked too."

"How much does a jilpoke cost?"

"I don't know that there's such a thing." He laughed. "You jilpoke a shed up with boards."

She ate her berries through the hole that was her mouth. If she opened it wide, she'd crack the calamine lotion.

"You ought to take a soda bath." He sipped his tea. "Throw in a whole box."

She touched her face. "On Halloween, I used to wear a hobo mask."

"One Halloween, in home, they dragged me out of the house." He stared down at the table. "Some girls. They took off my clothes."

Compassion flooded her, followed by rage at the girls who'd humiliated him.

He got to his feet. "Come fall, if we're still alive and thrashing, I'll dig up a patch of ground for your bulbs."

"Make sure you got the money," said June.

Hazel checked her purse as the bus carried them out of Fingabog Siding. Each member of the class give her sixty cents to get the gift for Mrs. McFee. Nothing too big-shot. Just a little something to show everyone's appreciation, a pair of pinking shears.

They rode past Patterson's farm, stacked with hay.

"Don't it smell grand?" sniffed June.

Hazel knew what she meant. Them first rolls in the hay when you was young and ignorant. Cousin Eddie'd been the first. That was probably why she always kind of figured on marrying him.

"Takes you back, don't it?"

Hazel agreed. There was nothing like being young for feeling randy all the time. Course, Bliss knew how to please her, more-so than Cousin Eddie, but a person slowed down. Her and Eddie was just like goats, always tumbling each other, pulling their shorts off behind every haystack. They even did it in the outhouse, with clothespins on their nose.

"If a person could bottle the smell of new-cut hay."

"They'd make a fortune," said Hazel. She'd buy a jar of it and put some on in the evening, to get herself more in the mood like.

But where would be the good if she married Eddie? It would have ended up the same; grown people just didn't need it as much. It would have ended up a far sight worse, if she looked at it truthful, with nothing to show but a batch of kids and a yardful of beer cans.

"Temperance Hollow," announced June.

Hazel looked out the windows. She'd heard them say, *the older the ram, the stiffer the horn,* but that was a lie made up by some old buck. Being young was lovely. She'd rather be twelve any day, when it come to certain things.

"There's Shyola Dixon's shack."

"I went to school with Shyola."

"Is that so?" asked June.

Now Shyola was an odd one. The man she lived with was eighty-nine and the one before, who died, was ninety-one. A nice-looking girl too. It was just a quirk she had. "Yes, Shyola's from Burnt Mill."

"I don't know much about her," said June.

Hazel could see June was fishing, but what could she tell her about Shyola? She didn't understand it no more than June did. "There's no accounting for taste."

"Pedico Village."

So it was. There was the smoke and the bricks. And

there was O'Haras' house down by the tracks. "Good welfare people."

"That's the size of it," said June.

"I wouldn't be surprised if they had a color TV."

"They do. Avery's sister knows them."

That settled it. She would have one by Christmas or bust. "Do they have a dryer?"

"Likely."

There was something wrong with the government. Everybody said so, and the O'Haras was the proof.

They crossed the bridge; both women smoothed their dresses.

"This weather's terrible on the hair."

"I can't gripe," said June, patting her curls.

Wouldn't it be something to be born with curls and never need no perm.

Front Street baked in the sun. There was the shops, the movie house, the terminal.

"Where do you think we ought to get them?"

"How about Singer's?"

"We want to get good ones now."

"Maybe Mongolian's Trimmings."

"Let's try Mongolian's Trimmings first."

They shouldered their bags and headed east. "Do you think she might already have pinking shears?"

"She never brought them to class."

"I guess we better stick to what's been voted."

"She can always take them back."

Hazel liked walking on Front Street with June, both of them decked out in flowered dresses. June was the youngest, but Hazel had more body to her. An attractive set of girls, should anyone care to notice. She stopped in front of the bank to fan her face. "Heat's killing."

"Be air conditioned in Mongolian's Trimmings."

They marched on.

"Look at that! They're closed."

"Closed for vacation. Ain't that something?"

"I guess it's Singer's."

They about-faced and crossed the street. The windows was brim-up with sales. Maybe after the pinking shears, they'd do a bit of shopping for themselves.

"Look at the sunsuit."

"You'd look cute in it," said Hazel. "I'm too hefty."

"You're nicely stacked," said June.

She was a lovely girl.

"Singer's is open anyways."

"Can I help you, ladies?"

"We'd like to see your pinking shears."

"I'm sorry, we're out of pinking shears at the moment. If you come back next week, we'll probably have them then."

"We need them today."

"Have you tried Margolin's Trimmings?"

"Mongolian's is closed for vacation."

"Perhaps you'll find a pair at the K-Mart."

"We don't want no cheap pinking shears."

"I don't know where else to suggest."

"Well, thank you." There it was. They'd have to go up to the K. "Shall we call a cab?" asked Hazel.

"I hate to spend the money." June thought a minute. "Let's hitch."

"I don't think Bliss would like it."

"I won't tell." She was out in the street, pointing her little thumb out.

A sort of racy car stopped right in front of them. "Where you going, girls?" The radio was pure blaring.

"Up to the K," said June.

Hazel wasn't too sure she liked the looks of them boys in the car.

"That's where we're going too." One of the boys got out, letting June in front and sitting himself in back with Hazel.

"Out doing some shopping?"

"Yes we are," said June.

Hazel was quite surprised to see how close June sat to her boy. As for herself, she set her bag on her lap and kept her knees together.

"What's your name?"

"June Smith." How quick that come out of June's mouth! "And that's my sister, Hazel."

"Hi, sister Hazel." Her boy was getting closer to her. Hazel could smell the beer on his breath.

She tightened her grip on her handbag.

"My name's Dick."

"Pleased to meet you, I'm sure."

He put his arm around her; she moved away.

June, up front, was in the self-same pickle, but she didn't appear to mind none.

"Come on, sister."

"My name's Hazel," Hazel repeated.

The boy up front must've been telling jokes to June, cause she was giggling under his arm.

"We're off to buy some pinking shears," said Hazel loudly.

Dick put his hand on her leg.

Land, what was a party to do, with June there getting so riled in front.

She pushed Dick's hand off her leg.

"Goddamn."

"I don't believe in language," said Hazel stiffly.

Dick tried to catch hold of her breast, but she twisted out of his reach.

The way June was wiggling up front, Hazel could swear that boy had his fingers clear under her bum. It sure made her think of them old days, but she wasn't no flippety girl no more. She was a legal married woman. "There's the K!" she shouted.

"You don't want to go there, do you?"

"Yes I do. Don't we, June."

"I don't care."

"We got to get them shears, June, and catch the two-thirty bus back."

"Bitch."

Nasty! "I'm getting off," said Hazel.

"I guess I am too," said June.

"You sure?"

"Yes," said Hazel. Nasty was the word; he was opening the door and pushing her out on the pavement.

June came tumbling after.

"They didn't even take us into the lot."

They walked across the road to the K-Mart.

"Cheaper than a cab anyways."

"Cheaper all right," said Hazel. It wasn't so easy for her to catch her breath after all that mauling. June appeared to be more used to it.

"I always hitch when I'm on my own."

"I never," said Hazel.

They entered the store, and headed for notions.

"I think I'll go to the ladies'," said Hazel. She wanted to think for a minute. This was another highlight on June.

She fixed her hair in the mirror. Who knew for sure that Gordy Colpitts was the father of June's baby, if she hitched all the time in Town? It might be anybody.

Hazel was glad she knew who her children's father was. They both looked exactly like Bliss.

Names didn't mean a thing. Who did a child resemble, that was the sure-tell. June's baby was still awful young, but they'd know for a fact when he took to walking. If he didn't toe out, he wasn't a Colpitts.

110

Bliss climbed down from the roof and flung his paint brush on the grass. "That should do her for another ten years."

His skin was now the same golden brown as his hair, and he reminded her of a lion.

They sat on the doorstep, his naked shoulder almost touching her. "Next week's my vacation."

Of course he had to have a vacation. There was no reason for her stomach to sink. "Are you going away?"

"I might do some fishing." He rolled a cigarette. "I'll keep working here evenings."

"You don't have to."

"I'd just as soon."

They looked out over the weeds, blooming now with wild carrot, pink clover and daisies.

"Would you like me to bring your tea outside?"

"No rush," he said.

She let the moment hang between them, neither work nor tea, but something outside the pattern they'd created. She glanced at his arm resting next to hers. The burnished fur was spattered with aluminum paint.

"I brought something to show you." He stretched to his feet, and ambled over to the Bluebird.

His evening shadow was enormous. What could he have to show her? She mocked her heart's excitement with mundane explanations: Samples of siding for the house. Wallpaper.

He returned to her carrying a small tin box. It was an old Swee-Touch-Nee tea chest, red and tarnished gilt.

He sat down and opened the lid, revealing a stack of cards and folded papers.

"This here's us in home." He handed her a ragged photograph of half a dozen children standing in a field. "That's me at the end."

She held the picture up to the light. It was as she'd imagined them: Bliss with his round head and surprised ears, the desolate bright field, the sisters.

He pointed, grazing her hand with his. "That's Patsy, and that's Sally, died of pneumonia, and that's Bob and Frank and Stewart."

They gazed at the faded photograph, and then he gave her another.

"Mom and Dad." The man was built like Bliss, with powerful neck and shoulders. The woman was small and tired in a limp cotton dress. They stood in front of a barn, staring solemnly at the camera.

"This here's Woolly." It was a dog in front of a sled. "Janie bent it all up."

112

The next was a pine tree split down the middle. "Hit by lightning." He put the pine tree back. "Dad cut it down after that. He was afraid it would fall on the house."

"Do you have a picture of the house?"

"It ain't a very good picture." The house was ramshackle, run-down, with a blurred shape on the porch. "That's our cat, but he wouldn't stand still."

He showed her the horse and the chickens pecking in front of a hen house. There were two pigs rubbing their snouts against a fence, another cat, a goat who belonged to some neighbors.

The fullness of the old time overflowed the photographs, warming Leona's barren dooryard, although the night was turning chilly. Bliss put on his shirt, brushing against her on the step.

"This was the school treat." Thirty kids or so squeezed together into the photograph.

"There you are." She found him.

He took out another group picture.

"Who are they?"

"I don't know. This was Dad's box, see."

"Are there any of Janie and Joey? Or Hazel?"

"Here's our wedding picture."

She opened herself to the worst.

The young man and girl stood in front of another ramshackle farmhouse, not dissimilar from the first. Bliss's hair was flattened down with water, his jacket was too tight to button and his grin was so foolish she wanted to cry. Hazel had her arm through his. She was young, younger than Bliss, with large high breasts and dimples. Leona held the picture up; her pain sharpened the image, which was slightly out of focus. The bride wasn't beautiful, but there was something about her, something mischievous and winning. Her black hair was frizzed in a perm and her slip was showing.

"She's very pretty."

"The lady who comes to the K-Mart took some pictures of Janie and Joey, big color pictures, but they're hanging on the wall." He emptied the tin on his lap. "This here's a poem Dad cut out of the *Courier*."

> Come all young men and I'll tell you
> Of a wrong that was did to me,
> By a man named Harvey Trehome
> And a girl who was engaged to me.

She read down the yellow newsprint. Some of the words had worn off the paper; the whole thing ran twenty-eight verses, from the betrothal to the double murder and the prison repentance.

> Come all you brave young country lads,
> A warning take from me,
> Never to murder the girl you love
> Whoever she may be,
>
> For if you do, you'll surely ruin
> And fine yourself like me
> And die a public scandal
> Upon the gallows tree.

"That's quite a poem too, ain't it?"
"Is it true?"
"Dad always said it was."
"What else is there?"
"Old papers." There was a receipt for a barrel of nails, half a raffle ticket, a report card for Bliss Dawson.
"You fell asleep in class?"
"Yup."
"Needs improvement in penmanship."
"And everything else," he added.
"How does Janie do in school?"

"Good," he said. "Damn good for all the help me and Hazel can give her."

She handed the report card to him and watched while he carefully fitted everything back in the tin.

He stood with the old tea box. "I'll get the donuts now."

She waited for him, and they went into the shack together.

"Do you have any pictures, Leona?"

"No," she answered. "Yes. I have one picture." She went to the shelf and took down a slim book. "This was my teacher."

"He writes books too?"

"Yes."

Bliss studied the face on the jacket, furrowing his brow. "You fancied him, did you?"

She nodded.

He walked over to the shelf and put the book back in its place.

She stood with her hands loose at her sides, watching him, until he reminded her softly, "You was going to get the tea."

"Did you hear?" Hazel walked into June's kitchen. "The *Courier's* going to be there."

"At the sewing class?"

"They're sending a photographer."

"I knew I should've touched my hair up!" Hazel fluffed out her wig. "How do I look?"

"Just like Emmeline from the TV."

"Go on!"

"You do."

"Emmeline's thinner."

"Not that much."

"Quite a bit." Hazel tried to pull her belly in.

"I wouldn't mind having a little of your bust."

116

A person could say what they liked about June Setzer, but she wasn't one to choke on a compliment.

June poured tea for her guest. "Your dress come out perfect."

"There's a few mistakes," admitted Hazel, "but I don't think nobody'd notice."

"Looks exactly like store-bought to me."

"How'd yours come out?" June was still wearing the muumuu she lounged about the house in.

"All but the zipper. It puckers."

"They won't take pictures of our back."

"I don't suppose." June sat down at the table. "Have some oatmeal cookies."

"You're a good cookie maker."

"Thank you."

"It's the truth." Hazel crunched her cookie earnestly. "I wonder how my dress will look in black and white."

"They'll all look gray, most likely."

"Some of them"—June bit off a piece of cookie—"really ain't fit to be in the *Courier*."

"Did you see the sleeves on Ethel's?"

"They look as if she put them on backwards."

"That's what I think she did."

"Maybe they'll edge her out of the picture."

"They ought to edge quite a few out."

"Do you suppose Mrs. McFee knew they was going to send the *Courier*?"

"I don't think it, or she would've been a lot stricter."

"It's her lookout."

"I hope she likes them pinking shears."

"We owe the rest of them four cents apiece. Avery figured it up for me."

"Hardly worth handing out."

"Doesn't half pay for our carfare."

"I don't think we need bother."

"They would have cost more if we got them to Mongolian's."

"Everything's more to Mongolian's."

"Did you wrap them nice?"

"Look." Hazel took the package out of her bag. "I thought pink for pinking shears."

"That's right too." June touched the shiny pink bow.

Hazel put it back in her bag. "Bliss's taking his vacation next week."

"So's Avery."

"Maybe we can go on a spree together."

"I been wanting to get up to that new shopping mall in Kouchilor."

"So have I."

"Well there. We can make a regular party of it."

"I'd like to get over to that Green's down Dungavesh."

"Supposed to be good, is it?"

"That's what I hear tell."

"We got a whole week, might as well do them both."

"Think we can get as far as Inkertown?"

"If we start out early enough."

"They got some beautiful stores over Inkertown."

"Have another cookie."

Hazel helped herself to another cookie. "I haven't been over Inkertown since Uncle Clyde was buried."

"He was buried in Inkertown, was he?"

"No, he was buried in Nebagonis, but we thought since we got that far, we might as well go on to Inkertown."

"I should get ready," said June.

They went into the bedroom, Hazel stopping to turn up the sound on the TV so they wouldn't miss anything important.

"Got your dress laid out, I see."

"Pressed it this morning." June slipped off her muumuu and stepped into her dress.

Hazel zipped it up. "It suits you."

"Do you think so?" June twirled around, letting her skirt flare out.

"No one would ever guess you done it on a second-hand sewer."

"It don't show too much puckering around the zipper?"

"Hardly notice."

"Your zip's perfect," said June. "Must be that new zig-zag of yours makes the difference."

Hazel gave a modest grunt. The fact of the act was she had Mabel put in the zipper.

June brushed her hair. "At least my sleeves are in right."

"What they might do is wedge Ethel between two other girls."

"I suppose them photographers is used to wedging people to get a picture right."

"I hope it."

"So do I. It ain't just the sewing class, it's all Fingabog we got to think of."

Leona stood in her doorway and admitted the possibility that the friendly interest she had in her carpenter was not altogether business.

In fact, he was looming so large in her life, she had little interest in anything else.

How could such a thing have happened?

She was a woman of culture. More—a scholar whose star was the intellect, intricate and wonderful; her sport was Shakespeare's flash of wit, the breathtaking turn of an image, Donne's metaphysics. She understood Christopher Smart, for God's sake!

Bliss was one step from illiterate. He was a bumpkin, a

brute, a hillbilly. He was married. His front tooth was missing.

The Bluebird chugged down the lane.

The bumpkin lumbered out with a long tube of rolled-up paper.

"What did you bring?"

"It's an inch-to-the-mile map I got on my lunch hour." He unrolled it on the grass, and she crouched down beside him, on her hands and knees.

"This here's Micwam Brook. I'll be fishing it next week." He broke into a dazzling grin. "I been thinking on it for years; I figure I might as well try it." He fixed himself a cigarette.

"It looks like it's all woods there." She ran her hand over the paper. "I hope you carry a compass."

"I don't need no compass." He laughed through his smoke. "And don't go calling the boy scouts up to find me if I'm late."

"What will you fish for?"

"Trout." They examined the map. "I bet you'd like fishing, Leona."

"I've never tried it."

"You just set and listen to the birds, and sometimes you see a fish flashing his colors, and if you catch him you can eat him, and if you don't, it don't matter, cause you like it just being out there. . . . You'd be good too. You ain't one to fidget and yak all the time."

She smiled. "I wouldn't know the first thing about fishing."

"You wouldn't have to. I'd show you everything."

The inch-to-the-mile map swam before her eyes.

"What I mean"—he was coughing and swatting flies—"is if we was kids together, like back in home, then I would've showed you everything. That's what I meant."

"If we were kids?"

"Like if you was my sister Patsy."

"Did you show her how to fish?"

"She never fished much, Patsy."

"Did Sally?"

"No."

She put the tip of her finger on the Micwam. "What else would we do?"

"You could pick raspberries if you wanted. They'd be out now. Raspberries is easier to pick than strawberries."

"And if it stormed while we were fishing?"

"If it stormed"—he had some trouble with his ash, which ended up on the Micwam—"we'd have to stay at the camp."

They remained hunched side by side, like a pair of greyhounds waiting for the signal to start.

It came with a gust of wind, blowing the paper up against them.

"Here's our storm." He rolled the map back into a tube. "I'd best get to work."

Bang, bang, bang, it rang, over the sound of Young Tony Andrews, the sound of Bliss's hammer drilling post-holes into the ground.

Hazel perked up her ears; the hammering stopped.

She went to the shed and opened her clothesline window, snapped it shut. It was that Avery again out there talking to Bliss. The two of them lighting up cigarettes. It wasn't right, everyone seeing the men so friendly; people would think the fence was all her idea.

She checked Joey in his crib, and crossed the bushes to Mabel's house. The only way to win against gossip was to set the record straight.

"Hello, Hazel."

"Lo, Mabel."

"Won't you come in?"

"Don't mind if I do."

"Have a seat." The old woman took her own in front of the treadle. The wall above the sewer was covered with photographs of grandchildren, great-grandchildren, and one of Janie and Joey.

"Lovely day, ain't it?"

"Nice day for working outside."

Hazel agreed. "That's why Bliss took the opportunity to start the fence."

"I noticed him putting post-holes in."

"We thought it would be for the best."

"I figured you'd be peeved as soon as I seen the picture."

"That fence ain't got nothing to do with no picture."

"It don't?"

"Course not."

Mabel fetched a newspaper clipping from her dresser. "This here's the picture I had in mind."

"I know what picture you had in mind."

"Cause you both bought them shears. I remember the day you went."

"I couldn't care less if June got her picture in the *Courier* giving them shears to Mrs. McFee, with me cut off at the hand. Why should I give a rusty?"

"You don't give a rusty?"

"No." Hazel tossed her head. "Although to my way of thinking, it would have been more of a picture with the whole class instead of just one person."

"Mrs. McFee looks good, don't she."

"She looks like she always looks."

"A nice-looking woman," said Mabel. "June looks good too."

"Each to her own taste."

"It is a pity though. Your dress come out so pretty."

"The *Courier* must not have thought so."

"I can't imagine. The way I figure it, the picture slipped in the printing."

"It ain't crooked, is it?"

"It must have slipped sideways," said Mabel. "Straight over like."

"Anyways, it don't matter to me none." Hazel turned to the TV. Young Tony Andrews and Emmeline was having it out again, but all you could see today was wiggly lines. Something was wrong with Mabel's picture tube, had been that way for years, one day snow, another day stripes.

"So that ain't why Bliss is putting up a fence?"

Hazel laughed loudly. "What an idea!"

"Fooled me."

"I'll tell you the reason." Hazel pulled her chair in toward the old woman. "But it's just between you and me, right?"

Mabel cocked her head forward.

"See," began Hazel, "we been thinking for some time, how will it be when the kids get older?"

"Joey and Donny?"

"We was thinking more of Janie. She's only going into second grade now, but soon enough she'll be up in sixth, seventh, busing off to junior high school. She'll have to know how to act, take care of herself, behave, if you know what I mean."

"What's that got to do with a fence?"

"It ain't so much the fence as who's behind it." She liked the sound of that. "Who's behind it is the problem. Little girls act like their elders, don't they? Kids are like monkeys— monkey see, monkey does."

"You don't want Janie acting like June?"

"You hit it on the head."

"But you was always friends with June."

"A person got to think to the future. See here, Mabel,

125

it's all right for me and you to overlook the way June behaves cause we're grown up and we know how to act ourself."

"She always appeared to behave good to me."

"What about Gordy Colpitts from down Dribley?"

"We don't know for sure about that."

"What if we seen it with our own eyes?"

"You didn't!"

"Not with Gordy Colpitts."

"With somebody else?"

"I ain't saying no further."

"You seen June Setzer with somebody else?"

"I ain't one to blaspheme my neighbor."

"Who was it?"

"What's that you're sewing?"

"This?" Mabel picked up the cloth in her machine. "This here's a dress for Gloriana, my Susan's youngest." She looked at the dress as if trying to remember something. "June Setzer with somebody else?"

"I shouldn't have said it," said Hazel.

"You can trust me."

"It ain't our business."

"But you're building a fence."

"There's plenty other reasons for that."

"What else?"

"A few things. For an instance, do you recall when old Mrs. Setzer was stopping?"

"She stopped half the spring and summer."

"Do you know June let her speak against Joey?"

"Joey? Our little Joey?"

"The same."

"What could anyone say about such a good baby?"

"She 'sinuated as much as said."

"She 'sinuated against little Joey?"

"That's correct."

Mabel got to her feet and put her face to the picture on the wall. "Janie and Joey is both perfect children."

"Not according to Mrs. Setzer."

"What could she say about them?"

"She 'sinuated that Janie was running the roads like a wild child and that Joey wasn't fit to stay with little Donny."

Mabel patted a large cat that leaped into her lap. "I heard everything now."

"You know Janie don't run the roads no more than anyone else. And as for Joey not being fit to stay with Donny . . ." Hazel snorted.

"All I can say"—Mabel smoothed the cat's mangy fur—"is that old Mrs. Setzer don't know a good child when she sees one."

"So that is why." Hazel got to her feet. "And if anybody tells you Bliss is building that fence cause I'm sore about not having my picture in the *Courier* giving some old pinking shears to Mrs. McFee, you can laugh right in their face."

"A fence is a big job."

"It's that, but it has to be done." Hazel walked to the door. "It's a blessing, in a way, that Bliss got his vacation this week. It's more like a confirmation from God."

"I don't know about God."

Hazel changed her tack; Mabel was never too religious. "It's handy is what it is."

"Yes."

"So you'll know what to say?" Hazel could see Mabel trying to get it straight in her head. "As long as you say it ain't got nothing to do with that picture."

"I thought I heard Avery out there helping him a while back."

"More likely borrowing something."

"It sounded from here like two hammers was going."

"If Avery wants to help, he can go right ahead."

"What about the butternut tree?"

Hazel chewed her lips thoughtfully. "We'll probably leave it open."

"It would be a shame to fence it off."

"And let them have all the nuts."

The cat jumped down, and Mabel got to her feet. "Ain't that Avery out there helping Bliss?"

The women walked to the dooryard. They could see the two men hammering.

"Well, it's Avery's vacation too."

Thirteen, that was a dozen corn at Tupper's. Leona covered her basket, and shambled down the road.

The dog days of August were on them, bleaching the fields and drying the streams.

A horn sounded and brakes screeched to a stop beside her. "Hop in, baby!"

She looked up, flustered.

"Who did you think it was?" He was chuckling at his joke, pushing open the door of the Bluebird to let her get in beside him.

"How did you know I was here?"

"I know everything in your head."

"Do you?"

"As far as grade six." He steered right on Sussex Avenue.

"Tell me the truth, how did you know I was at Tupper's?"

"I felt like a feed of corn."

They turned left on Alling, left down Farrier Lane.

She took her basket into the house, and Bliss unloaded the trunk of his car.

Each day he brought another load of shingles from "some old feller's barn." The old fellow had charged them ten dollars for the shingles, and Bliss charged her three dollars a load.

It had been his idea to use old shingles "so as to match the ones you got." He'd found the barn, made the deal, and was nailing each one into place.

Occasionally she thought of the day when there'd be no more work on the shack. It would be her freedom, the end of her ridiculous infatuation. But she didn't dwell on the idea, for in the meantime—there he was, standing outside, hammering shingles.

Sometimes a shingle would crack, and he'd toss it to the ground, shaking his head at the waste. She wished they all would crack so, like Penelope, he'd go on tacking shingles up night after endless night.

Any old shingles that he took off the house went into the shed along with the cracked ones, "for kindling," he said. He was going to get hardwood too, and split it, and put in a Franklin fireplace, "to make it cozy in winter."

"I don't know how to start a fire."

"I'll show you."

She'd left it at that.

"Leona."

"What?" She opened the door.

"I seen an old Franklin laying in someone's shed."

"Is it for sale?"

"He'll sell it. How much do you want to offer?"

"What do you think?"

"We'll start at five."

"He'd never sell it for five."

"Didn't we get a whole barn for ten?" He picked up another shingle. "We'll go as high as fifteen."

She sat down on the step. "Do you have a Franklin in your house?"

"We ain't got no time to look at a fireplace. TV's always on." He took some nails from his pocket. "Besides, the old woman uses nine cord of wood just for cooking." He held the shingle in place. "Course it ain't only the wood that makes her bread so good."

"Will she enter the fair this year?"

"Yup." He drove a nail through the shingle. "Labor Day weekend. You ought to go up."

"I don't think so."

"You'd have fun." He pried off a rotten shingle. "Ferris wheel, cotton fluff, get to see the fancywork."

She hugged her knees to her chin. "What can I enter in the fair?"

"Enter a book. Why not?" He put down his hammer and took out tobacco and paper. "No one else will enter a book. You're bound to win first place."

She watched him roll his cigarette. Now he'll come and sit beside me.

He came and sat beside her.

She felt her desire rising. She could practically chart his proximity by the tides inside her. These moments on the step when their bodies almost touched and they could hear each other breathing were high tide.

He puffed on his cigarette.

She looked down at their legs, both in baggy pants, and their big boots.

131

"House is shaping up, ain't it."

"It really will be a cottage soon."

"All you'll need is some flowers."

"I hate the thought of its shaping up!"

He stared open-mouthed at her outburst, then escaped in a fit of coughing.

Why did I say such a stupid thing!

"That's okay." He reached his hand to hers but drew it quickly away. "I know what you mean. It's the work that's the pleasure. Once it's finished, what have you got? Still only a place to lay your head. I felt the same about finishing our house."

She sat in stunned silence, feeling the imprint of his hand on hers.

"Leona . . . Would you like me to get you a kitten? I know where I can get one for free. A real clean kitten."

"A kitten?"

"You know. For company."

She started to laugh and felt her laugh verging on tears. She floundered to her feet. "I'd better clean the corn."

She went into the shack, and husked the ears, stripping off the jackets and the fine silk tassels. There was a worm in one; she took it to the door, and blew him onto the grass.

"I never heard tell of anyone making a wish on a worm before."

"Here's another one." She went to his side with the corn. "Make your wish."

"My wish?" He turned away from the corn and picked up a shingle. "A man gets in trouble thinking wishful thoughts."

She blew off the second worm.

"What did you wish for, Leona?"

"I wished that I could be like Bliss Dawson and never have any wishful thoughts."

He laughed. "Now that poor worm's carrying a lie on his

back." He struck the shingle with his hammer. "You don't want to have thoughts like I do."

"I'd trade with you any day."

"Funny if you did"—he picked up another shingle—"and found you got the same thing you traded."

"Can I go on the Ferris wheel?" demanded Janie.

"If the lines ain't too long," said Hazel.

"How soon will we get there?"

"Another five minutes," said Bliss.

"I'm going to be sick."

Hazel turned around in her seat. "You better not be!"

"I better have some gum."

"Here."

"Don't we have no Juicy Fruit?"

A car passed, honking; Bliss honked back. "Derwin Gaffey."

"I dare say everyone will be there."

"Everyone in the world?" asked Janie.

"She sure gets overexcited."

"We'll be there in two more minutes," said Bliss.

They were crossing the Sourgrass Bridge.

"Look at all the people walking to the fair!" squealed Janie.

"Be good now." Hazel smoothed her dress. "Did Joey dirty himself?"

Janie touched her brother's bottom. "No."

"Lot's crowded." The two-tone car waited in line.

"Hey Bliss!"

"Royden!"

"I see the little lady took second in donuts."

"And honorable for brown bread."

"Brown bread too. Didn't notice. Well, see you later."

"See you, Royden."

"Royden don't look so good," said Hazel.

They inched up to the ticket booth. "Two and two please, Mrs. Carter."

"Brought the baby, did you? Ain't he a big one now. And this is little Junie, ain't it?"

"Janie."

"Little Janie. Ain't that nice. I seen your donut, Mrs. Dawson."

Hazel smiled. "Great crowd today."

"Must be the weather."

They found a parking place in the lot.

"There's the Ferris wheel," shrieked Janie.

"You wait up for us! I don't want to lose no children." Hazel was strapping Joey into his stroller.

"Hello, Bliss."

"Wayne."

"Lo, Mrs. Dawson."

"Lovely day."

"I want some cotton fluff!"

135

"Howdy, Bliss."

"Alvin."

"Mrs. Dawson."

"Quite a crowd."

"Can I have money for fluff?"

Bliss dug into his pocket.

"Get some for us too," said Hazel.

"You entering the splitting contest this year, Bliss?"

"Yourself?"

"I might. Young Douglas won the corn boil."

"Did we miss the corn boil?"

"Chain saws going on now."

"Here's your fluff."

"Don't get none on your dress."

The party continued forward.

"Ain't that old Mrs. Nagle?"

"Gotten awful bent up, hasn't she?"

"Hey Bliss."

"Luther."

"Seen your donut, Mrs. Dawson."

"Janie, stop stepping on my feet."

"Can I ride the Ferris wheel?"

"We're going to watch the chain-saw contest."

"There's the Crown and Anchor," said Bliss.

Hazel sniffed. "They shouldn't really allow no betting here."

"Hazel Dawson!"

"Ida Potts!"

"And Janie. Now ain't that cute, mother-and-daughter dresses. And little Bliss, he's sure a big one."

"Little Joey."

"That's right."

"Where's your crowd?"

"I lost them somewhere. Hal's at the Crown and Anchor.

Sadie's looking at the fancywork. The kids are onto the wheel."

"I want to go on the wheel."

"I seen your donut. My ring won third in tea cakes. Alice Sturdge took rolls. And the quilts are just lovely this year. There's some baby quilts never been entered in the fair before."

"See you later, Ida, we're going to watch the chain saws."

"Over by now, likely."

"Then I can go on the Ferris wheel!"

"The lines at the wheel are terrible. Bye now, Hazel."

They pushed forward.

"Bliss and Hazel!"

"Lo, Fred. Lo, Rhoda."

"Rhoda's pale," said Hazel.

"See, the chain saws are over! Now can I go on the wheel?"

"You come with us! We got to show our faces at the donuts."

"Don't even get to eat them."

"How you doing, Bliss?"

"The very best. And you, Lloyd?"

"Can't complain."

"Who won the chain saws?"

"It won't take long," said Hazel, hauling Janie along, "just a couple of minutes to show we care."

They went into the exhibition hall.

"If it ain't Hazel Dawson!"

"Maggie Doak!"

"Lovely day."

"Great crowd."

"I seen your donut."

"Showing your afghans this year?"

"Joey dirtied himself."

"Hush, Janie."

"I want to go on the Ferris wheel!"

Leona wore her heather suit and the beige silk shirt which opened at the throat, showing her collarbones.

In a fit of fury at her hair, she'd snipped it off; now it hung about her face like jagged strips of cloth.

The bus wasn't crowded, in spite of the holiday. She realized with alarm that people from town didn't go to the Sourgrass Fair. It would be strictly north boondocks.

As they wound along the highway, the houses grew more sparse, changing from bungalows to shacks, trailers, isolated farms. The hay rose in fragrant mounds. Cows grazed lazily in the grass. A black and white cat sunned on his doorstep.

They drove through little villages, stopping to let people on and off. One of the stops must have been Fingabog Siding, but she couldn't tell which. She might not even know when they got to Sourgrass.

Long bus rides made her nauseated. She closed her eyes, tried to breathe through her mouth.

She would have to go to the end of her ticket, but then she could turn around, catch the next bus back and avoid the misery ahead. Why do I want to be a spectacle at some country fair? For the sake of seeing him with his family? Am I such a glutton for punishment? Or do I hope he might say hello? Or that I might win a dish at Bingo?

"Sourgrass Fair."

Several of the passengers got off.

"Ain't you going to Sourgrass, ma'am?"

All eyes turned to Leona, who got to her feet and staggered forward, bumping her head as she went through the doorway.

"When's the next bus back?" she asked.

"I'll be coming through at seven," he smiled. "Gives you four hours."

"Thank you."

The bus took off, leaving her alone on a rickety bridge.

Sunlight glazed the water. The village seemed to be asleep, except for the few people who'd gotten off the bus and were plodding toward what must be Sourgrass and the fair.

She looked in the opposite direction. Beyond the highway was a hill, with thick woods, where she could hide herself and her folly until seven. If she met a bear she'd climb a tree, and if she met a moose she'd bark like a dog. Or was it the other way around?

"Miss deVos?"

She jumped.

A man, or a boy, a squat football-shaped idiot, stood blinking up at her from penetrating pig's eyes.

The two freaks stared at each other in the bright silence. Neither of them smiled.

"I'll show you where the fair is." He made a gesture with his crooked shoulder, and she followed him across the bridge.

"It's kind of you," she murmured.

"I seen your picture in the *Courier*."

They paraded past the frame houses, the post office, the little library—she and the idiot, the sideshow making its entrance. We ought to bang drums.

"I cut out the pictures, see, and paste them in a book."

In front of them was a gate with a gatekeeper in a booth.

"Mrs. Carter, I brung Miss deVos."

The woman tore off a ticket. "A dollar fifty, please."

The idiot was walking away.

"Thanks," called Leona.

He continued down the street.

Leona took out her money and handed it to the woman.

"You from Town?"

"Yes."

"Got quite a crowd today. Must be the weather."

Leona made her way to the parking lot; there was the Bluebird. But if she left, the woman at the booth would see her. And the idiot. She entered the fair.

There was no music, except for a thin rink-a-dink coming from the tiny Ferris wheel. There was one refreshment tent, a couple of booths, a barn from which protruded the hindquarters of a horse, and a battered wooden building marked EXHIBITION HALL.

A few dozen people wandered aimlessly about, carrying sticks of cotton candy.

Where is everybody?

They must be in the exhibition hall; she walked toward it.

Bliss appeared in the doorway, golden, laughing, pushing a baby stroller.

She ducked into the refreshment tent.

He was with a fat young woman with black frizzy hair and a little girl dressed to match the woman.

"What do you want?"

"Coke, please."

She laid her coins on the counter. She'd stay in the refreshment tent until they were out of sight.

They were stopped at one of the booths now, talking to a man there.

Yes, it was Hazel, the dimples and large high breasts, but fifty pounds heavier. She was still pretty though, and the beautiful little girl who clung to her hand showed what the mother once had been.

Leona sipped the fizzy drink. Now that she looked more closely, she saw Janie's dark coloring was deceptive; it was Bliss she took after, with her high cheek bones and full lips.

140

The Dawsons were moving on; Leona backed farther into the tent.

Janie was pulling at her mother's hand and demanding something. *Clop.* She got cuffed in the head.

They stopped to talk to another family.

The baby was Bliss too, in great buttery baby folds, smiling like a sleepy Roman emperor after the orgy.

Bliss was turned away from Leona; she put down her paper cup and dashed to the exhibition hall.

Inside, she caught her breath, among onions, pumpkins, potatoes, monstrous squash and foot-long green beans. Two or three old men looked up from their coughing.

She climbed the squeaking stair-boards.

A handful of women were upstairs, looking at the exhibits, and most of them seemed to be staff.

The walls were lined with quilts worked in formal patterns, mittens, doilies, tea towels, baby sweaters. Down the center of the hall were potted African violets and red geraniums, many with awards or honorable mentions.

The cases were on the left: pies, rolls, breads, cakes, donuts, muffins, cookies, tarts, tea rings, biscuits, fruit scones, jars of jelly, jam, pickled cucumber. She read the labels. *Donut, second prize, Mrs. Bliss Dawson, Fingabog Siding.* The famous donut lay on a piece of cardboard, a powdery ring of dough with a bite taken out of it. She moved her eyes down the case to *Donut, first prize.* The two donuts looked identical.

She must check out the breads. Wasn't it brown bread? *Brown bread, honorable ment., Mrs. Bliss Dawson, Fingabog Siding.*

What now? Three and a half hours. She dragged herself back to the quilts and tried to admire the circles, stars, geometric daisies, excruciatingly perfect stitches.

"Something, ain't they?"

"They're extraordinary."

"You from Town?"

Leona nodded down at the woman.

"Big crowd today."

"Where is everybody?"

"Out and around." The woman waved toward the show-cases, the potted plants. "There'll be turkey dinner later."

"I have to catch the bus back at seven."

"That don't matter. Turkey dinner starts at five. It's across the road in the church hall, but you hang on to your ticket, and they'll let you back in here for free."

"Thanks."

"Come back again now."

"I will." Leona walked down the stairs.

The old men looked up from their coughing.

She went to the door.

"Mommy, Mommy, there's a giant!"

"Don't point, Janie."

"Over there!"

"It's Miss deVos," said Bliss.

"Fancy that."

"Mommy, she's looking at us." Janie gripped both parents' hands.

"Well, ain't you going to make us acquainted?" Hazel elbowed her husband in the ribs.

Bliss coughed, and led the procession forward to Leona, who stood panic-stricken in front of the exhibition hall.

"Hello," she said.

"Afternoon."

Hazel stepped forward.

"This is my wife, Hazel Dawson."

"Pleased to meet you," managed Leona.

"The same I'm sure." Hazel showed her dimples. "I'd like

142

you to meet my children." She yanked Janie into the picture. "Janie, say hello to Miss deVos."

"Hello."

"Hello."

"This is our youngest, Joey."

Leona found her tongue. "He's a beautiful child."

"Takes after his father." Hazel tittered and Bliss scowled.

"I looked just the same," said Janie, "when I was a baby."

"Yes, she did," said Hazel.

"I can see. She's very pretty."

Janie snickered.

That seemed to be it. The Dawsons looked at Leona and at the ground. She looked at the ground and at the Dawsons.

"Lovely day," said Hazel.

"Lovely."

"Not too cool."

"No, it's just right."

"Big crowd."

"I want to go on the Ferris wheel."

"We're talking to Miss deVos."

"Don't let me keep you," said Leona.

"Seen the fancywork?"

"Oh! I saw your donut. Congratulations."

"You seen the bread?"

"Yes. It was a beautiful loaf of bread. I thought it was as nice as any of the winners."

"An awful lot's politics," admitted Hazel.

"Really?"

"It's a scandal, the exact same thing as government."

"Are you finished talking to Miss deVos?"

"Hush up, Janie. Them lines is too long at the wheel. We don't want to waste our time standing on no line."

"Would you like me to take her?"

"She don't need to go on the wheel. It's just an idea she has."

"I'd be glad to take her."

"Can she, Mommy? Huh?"

"I mean it," said Leona. "I'd like to go on myself."

"If you want to," shrugged Hazel. "But if she gets sassy, smack her."

"Come on." Janie tugged Leona's hand.

"Where will we find you afterward?" Leona called back to the parents.

"Give a hoot. We'll be around somewheres or another."

"Are you a giant, Miss deVos?"

"Well." Hazel stared after the two figures. "She sure is a homely-looking rig."

Bliss stooped over the stroller and got out Joey's bottle. "Here you are, feller."

"You think she'd do something with her hair."

"She did," said Bliss. "She cut it off."

"She needs a good perm."

"Don't you want your bottle, Joey?"

"I wonder exactly how tall she might be."

"Six foot one," said Bliss.

Hazel shook her head. "Couldn't really tell it from the *Courier*."

"There you go." Bliss got the bottle into his son's mouth.

"All bone and gristle too." Hazel looked around. "Ain't you going to win me something nice at ring-toss?"

The rain beat down on the steel roof, and thunder rumbled. Flashes of lightning cracked the sky, illuminating her yard in the darkness.

She stood in the window watching the storm tear through the trees, and longed for similar release.

Night fell early now, deepening the intimacy between the two people inside the shack.

She turned away from the violence outside to look at the Franklin and at Bliss, concentrated on his task of joining stovepipes together.

"They say a man has to go to church to work with stovepipes." He eased one pipe inside the other. "And I went once." He stood up in triumph, wiping his hands on his pants. "Now all we want's a fire."

They both made for the shed, bumping shoulders at the door and drawing back as though scorched.

"I'll get the wood."

"I can carry some of it."

They went through the door with care, offering each other plenty of leeway.

"Get a handful of shingles and a big piece of birch bark." He gathered the heavy lengths of hardwood himself.

They crouched in front of the stove.

"You put the bark in first, see, or a few sheets of the *Courier*, but since you don't get the *Courier*, we'll use the bark." He laid the shingles on next, angling them "for to get a good draft," and placed the split wood on top.

The bark caught first, crackling with a pale blue flame. He stood the screen in front of the fireplace.

"I'm sure I could do that."

"Ain't nothing to it." He sat back on the floor. "Nothing for to do but watch it, warm and cozy-like."

She sat back beside him.

The shingles caught, filling her nostrils with pungent cedar.

He rolled a cigarette. The shadows played on the planes of his face, turning him to sculpture.

The rain on the tin sounded like hoofbeats.

It was understood, without their speaking of it, that work on the shack would soon end. The days were too short and cold for working outside evenings; indoors there was nothing left but little chores they invented.

He leaned forward and removed the screen, threw another log on. "It will be nice for you to have a fire winter nights."

The rain increased in gusts, galloping across the tin,

hacking, coughing, muttering. "Can you hear voices in the rain?"

"Nope."

"I can't make them out," she said, "just angry mutterings."

"Must be your conscience."

"Why my conscience?"

"I don't know." He lay back with his head on his arm. "Maybe it's my conscience."

She wanted to lie down beside him but no longer trusted her own movements. Lately she seemed to be more disjointed than ever; she felt wrung out as a dishrag. Sometimes, alone, she cried for no reason.

"Leona."

"Yes?"

"That teacher you had. The one who writes them books."

"I haven't seen him in nine years."

"It ain't none of my business." He struggled through his smoke. "I don't know why I thought of him."

"He was my thesis advisor."

Bliss brushed Clem Stegmann away with his cigarette.

Lightning pierced the room, followed by thunder, which made the dishes tremble.

"I ought to be getting home."

"Do you want something to eat first?"

"No." He tossed his stub behind the screen, and lay down again, resting his weight on one elbow.

Their eyes met, and they looked away.

"If your oil heater gets broke, you can always burn wood. You'll never be cold."

"It's just what I needed."

"You can even cook on it in a pinch."

"I can bake potatoes in it."

"Potatoes is good that way."

She could feel his eyes on her again and was afraid to turn her head.

"Did he fancy you too?"

"Yes." She added truthfully, "In his way."

The rain was a gentle patter.

"Appears to be letting up." He looked at the ceiling. "Would be a good time for me to go."

The fire was burning low, and the room was almost in darkness.

"If I wait a bit longer, it might stop."

She nodded.

"That's what I'll do," he said.

They studied the glowing embers.

The Christmas sale book came.

Hazel went through it one page at a time, not letting herself skip right up to the good stuff, but going over each and every thing, from the lounging outfits on the cover, through new-and-novel gift ideas, toys, candy, fruitcakes, presents for loved ones across the ocean, lifetime trees, holiday wrappings, under-ten-dollar stocking stuffers, into women's fashions, where she put a chunk of wood in the stove and brewed herself a pot of tea, cause here's where she liked to dawdle.

She buttered a slice of bread and spread it thick with strawberry jam, just picturing herself in that there *chiffon-jacketed dress, ultra glamorous, nylon, hand wash, hang dry, peacock as shown, misses' 8 to 18.* She was a perfect eighteen, if she didn't gain from here to December.

She'd wear them goldy boots with it, *see description page 210.* She didn't turn ahead; she would read it when it come. Weren't they the thing though, two-inch platforms and laced clear up. You couldn't hop right into them boots.

She sipped her tea. Her wig would go real good with peacock blue.

She wet her thumb and turned the page. There now!

Fabulously fringed vest-dress with luxurious lacy look for those very special evenings. The very thing to wear to wrastling!

She tore her eyes away from the vest-dress to catch up with the story. Young Tony Andrews was undergoing one of them identity crisis things.

It was an awful tasty strawberry jam; she took another bite. She might look good in one of them long coats, *elegantly cut and heaped with opulent Eskilon pile.* Elegant was the word all right, but she wouldn't look too elegant if she tripped on her bum.

Car coats for the young suburban. That was her to a hair! This here wool one looked kind of cute; on the other hand, that there corduroy one was washable.

The telephone rang. Once, twice, three short ones. Somebody calling June.

Hazel picked it up.

"Hello, June, this is Stella."

"How are you?"

"Fine."

"Did you get your Christmas sale book?"

"I just picked it up at the post. You look at yours yet?"

"I'm in home appliances."

"Hold on a minute . . . okay. What page?"

"Two-eighty."

"Two-eighty. Got it."

"That dryer on the bottom."

"Multi-cycle fabric-master?"

"No, budget fabric-master."

"That one down in the corner? Lovely."

"I'm putting the order in this month. Any orders over two hundred put in before November wins you an almond-iced cake."

"It ain't over two hundred."

"Won't be much to make up the difference. It'd be a shame not to, considering the cake."

"Did Avery say you could have a dryer for Christmas?"

"Yes."

Hazel clicked off. Course Avery said so. He couldn't very well not, after he heard that Bliss got me one.

She looked over at the dryer setting beside the sink. It weren't no budget number neither.

She poured herself more tea. This Miss deVos's house was the longest odd job Bliss ever landed. Too bad it couldn't last forever. Everything had to end sometimes, but there might be a few more nice things to come out of it before it did.

Such as, for example, a color TV set. They put them clear in back of the book, and she wouldn't get to there till midnight, likely.

She turned to the story. She could put this old black-and-white set in the kids' room.

"Here's the money," said Tony.

"How'd you get it?" demanded Emmeline.

The organ music rose.

Where was she? Car coats.

Maybe she'd sneak a peek at the dryer June was going to get. It wasn't exactly cheating, cause she'd flip right back again. Page two-eighty. Multi-cycle fabric-master, budget fabric-master. $165. Not bad for a fabric-master. She read down the fine print. There you are—no sensitronic shut-off! I wouldn't take it if they give it to me free.

Back to car coats.

Doors banged.

"I'm home!"

"I hear you."

"What you looking at?" Janie slid under her mother's arm.

"Don't upset my tea!"

"The Christmas book!"

"You'll get it when I'm finished."

"Oh, Mommy, ain't that a nice coat?"

"Think it would suit me?"

"It would." Janie was tugging at the pages. "Can I just take a tiny little peek at the toys?"

"No."

Joey let out a wail.

Hazel got up.

Janie pounced on the book.

"Don't you lose my place."

"I won't. I'll keep my thumb right into it."

"Wash your hands first." Hazel went to the crib, and picked up her baby, sniffing his bottom. "It's dirty, ain't it."

He laughed and pulled her hair.

"Mommy, did you see the Wee Lady manicure kit?"

"What in ever would you do with a manicure kit?"

"My nails."

"They're all bit off." Hazel unpinned Joey's diaper.

"But it's just the same as they show on TV. Remember?" Janie brought the book over, shoving it under her mother's face.

Hazel dropped the diaper in the bucket and folded a new one.

"Does that say Wee Lady manicure kit?"

"Can't you read that much?" asked Hazel.

"I could, but I don't have the time."

"What are they teaching you in school? Here, give me that thing." She bent over the picture. "*Wee Lady.*"

"I knew it!" Janie turned back a page. "Here's a nice toy for Joey." She held it up in front of the baby. "Ain't that nice, Joey?"

He gave the toy a wallop.

"He'll rip it, and you'll get the strap!"

Janie took the book back to the table. "Wee Lady, oh Wee Lady . . ."

"Stop your singing. I can't hear Camilla Starr."

"Oh won't we be a hit, With our Wee Lady manicure kit!"

It had been no more than a chimera, an imaginary sonnet, a poem she'd come across and lost among the dusty volumes.

The work was done, she had her freedom and would never see him again.

She got up from her desk. Perhaps they'd meet on campus.

She walked down the stairs. And he might nod to her.

She started to go toward the gates, then went the other way, following the route she'd walked each evening with such anticipation, turning into the driveway that led behind the hothouses.

The lot was not quite empty. In the fading light, she

made out the shape of the Bluebird and a figure stretched out beneath it.

She shuffled over to the car.

"Leona?"

"Yes."

"I'd know your walk anywhere," he chuckled. "I'd know it on the moon, I bet."

"What're you fixing?"

"The tail pipe come off, see." His voice was muffled beneath the car. "I'm tying it up."

"Do you need any help?"

"I could use a flashlight is all."

His baggy pants protruded from the rusted bottom of the car—his belt, his pants, and his heavy boots.

She knelt beside him in the darkening shadows.

"Going to keep me company, are you?"

His legs were spread; his body squirmed as he fastened the tail pipe.

She put her hand on his fly.

All motion froze. There was no sound, not even a tremor of air, only her blood pounding in her ears.

The half man didn't stir.

She pulled down his zipper.

Her heart was going so fast it must surely break. People of thirty-four were known to have coronaries.

Tremulously she opened his snaps, and slipped her fingers inside his shorts; swiftly, furtively, in a race with her heart, she drew him forth.

How sad it was, this small limp thing, how fragile and vulnerable.

It rose between her palms, unsure, hesitant.

She prostrated herself completely, and laid her lips on its velvet tip.

The scent of Bliss wiped out what little sense was left in her head. She parted her lips, she knew she was mad, but his warmth was the months of their summer, and the racing of her heart was the ring of his hammer on shingles.

His body twitched, bumped against the car; particles of dirt rained down from the fender, settling on her hair. She'd been parched for so long, unable to reach out as other people do; she'd wanted so much to reach out to him and couldn't, until now, when he was nothing but a pair of trousers and a disembodied cock.

She moved her lips in a nightmare frenzy. How do I even know it's Bliss? It could be old Charlie Fudge, that's how little this resembles love, how little this mindless passion approaches my feeling for him; despair inflamed her further, and through her delirium, she caught the smell of axle grease.

He trembled. She swallowed. His smile, his thoughts, the months of their summer spurted down her throat in warm drafts.

Above her frenzy, she felt a shuddering, his choking breath beneath the Bluebird.

She drew her lips away.

He lay rigid, though his breathing was still audible.

The absence of speech or movement suddenly became awful.

The ugliness of her act engulfed her.

She scrambled to her feet, and fled from the parking lot, down the hill, through the gates, galloped along Sussex Avenue, trying to escape the sound of his breath beneath the car. She'd exploited his helplessness. She'd humiliated him, like the girls who'd dragged him from the house on Halloween.

She turned the corner on Alling, veering against her forward momentum, careened into space. Her hands shot out a second too late; the grain of the sidewalk was crystal clear as it struck her face.

She lay on her belly. For three dollars an hour, she'd betrayed him, after living for months like a vampire on his virility.

Blood ran from her nose, and she couldn't open one eye, but the scene repeated itself in her mind, her big fingers unsnapping his shorts, her ugly tongue brutalizing him.

She crawled to her feet. It must be plain to him now—all the work had been nothing but a lie, a deception contrived by a sex-starved spinster to get next to a man.

She limped down Farrier Lane to her shack. Mixed with the blood on her lips was the taste of his semen.

"It's only four hundred dollars, and if we pay before November, we get two almond-frosted cakes."

"It don't say two," corrected Bliss. "It says one for two hundred."

"Stands to reason they'd give you two for four hundred, don't it?"

"Where am I going to get four hundred dollars?"

"Land, you don't pay it all at a clip." She snapped the lunch pails shut.

"Miss deVos is a giant," said Janie.

"She ain't," said Bliss.

"She is. She told me she is."

"She's pretty close to," said Hazel.

"Finish your Sugar Crisps, Janie." Bliss pushed his own away. "I'll take you to school."

"You go to Linda's after school, hear? You ain't to come home till supper." Hazel spread Janie's hair away from her scalp.

"What're you doing?"

"Checking for nits."

"You're hurting me."

"I won't be home till five." She let Janie's hair fall forward. "Lord, these bridal showers are a nuisance."

"Don't go," said Bliss.

"Easy enough to say." She took his bowl away. "But one of these days Janie'll be getting married, and then it will all pay off."

"I ain't getting married."

"Everybody gets married."

"Miss deVos ain't married. I asked her."

"You want to be an old-maid schoolteacher?"

"I'm going to be a movie star like Emmeline."

"That might not be so bad."

"Get your books," said Bliss.

"I'm going to be on the TV set, and everyone's going to say how sweet I am."

"Sweet as a pickle," said Hazel.

"Bye, Joey!"

The doors banged shut behind them.

Peace and quiet, thought Hazel, turning up the sound on the TV.

She went and ran her bath. It's at a time like this that a person really needs more than just the one wig.

The water was nice and hot, and she sank down into it. All the girls at the shower seen her in the red one.

She wondered how she'd act when she come face to face with June. She heard them on the phone deciding which to

159

ask, her or June, and then they asked the both. She lathered her arms.

She'd be polite of course. No one could ever say she didn't know her breeding. She'd say good afternoon.

She rubbed the soap on her breasts, giving herself a good feel. She might even ask after little Donny. Lord knows Donny wasn't to blame.

She soaped her neck. And if June asked after Bliss, then she'd ask after Avery. She'd handle it tit for tat.

But there was one person she wouldn't ask after, and that was old Mrs. Setzer. That was carrying manners too far. She bent forward and soaped her feet, getting in between the toes.

The phone rang, two, three; June. A bad time for people to call each other, when she was into the tub. She washed her leg, stretching it out in the air, admiring the curve of it.

Maybe Janie would be a movie star. She sure has looks to spare, between me and Bliss. That would be something though.

Janie'd send home postal cards from Hollywood, New York, Paris, all them dangerous places, and everyone in Finga-bog would admire the cards hanging up on my wall. I might put them into a frame.

And I'd see her every day on the TV, like Camilla Starr. It was awful hard to think of Janie on the TV, grown up and going in for sin.

She stood up to wash her privates. Beauty could be a curse. Camilla Starr, for example. She lathered her hair with pleasure.

Camilla Starr did have lovely clothes though, white pantsuits and a white mohair coat. It would probably make Janie sneeze, a mohair coat. Wonder where the child gets all them allergies from. Me and Bliss don't have no allergies.

She sat back down and ran in a little more hot. In the Christmas book she seen a pillow for the bathtub.

What she'd really like—she let the water come up to her chin—was one of them bathroom telephones so she wouldn't miss out on news.

If Bliss worked in an office, more like Tom Flagerty, she could call him up from her tub. She'd lean back against her pillow, and they'd chit-chat for a while. *How is things in money orders? Not too bad, and how's your bath?*

Joey was calling. She heaved out of the water and dried herself with a towel. If she and Bliss had their own master bathroom, they'd have towels that said His and Hers.

Bliss was an awful hand for blackening towels; it was the work he did, plus always tinkering under the car. Tom Flagerty's wife probably never had to wash a towel, as far as the looks of it went.

Joey was yelling louder. Hazel tied on her terry robe and padded out to the crib. "Did you throw your bottle on the floor?"

He looked down through the rails at the bottle.

She bent to pick it up. She'd have to hunt out another sitter, since Mabel was going to the shower too. It was wonderful the way a woman as old as Mabel kept herself so lively, only it would be handier for baby-sitting if she ran with a different crowd.

161

She bent over the desk, searching for her lecture cards. She was five minutes late for her two o'clock class, but the desk was a wreckage of papers, and her head ached from her fall on Alling Street.

There was a knock on the door.

"Just a minute."

The door opened and shut. "I never fixed my car last night."

She turned and faced him with half a dozen speeches, all, she now saw, inadequate, locked in her throat.

"It was too dark to see any more," he said. "I had to hitchhike home."

"I'm so sorry."

"I'm just teasing," he grinned, walking toward her. "Wouldn't I have looked funny hitching the roads with my balls hanging out."

His arms were around her, and she felt everything slip away—her remorse, her conflict, her class.

"Excuse me for interrupting."

They drew apart.

"Your students are waiting," said Curdy.

She knew she should answer him, but all she could think of to say was that Bliss had held her, that he'd come to her and held her. And Curdy already knew that.

Bliss spoke. "Tell them she'll be a couple of minutes."

Curdy left, closing the door behind him. Something nagged at the edge of her mind, about a world she'd forgotten in Bliss's embrace, a world of compromising situations and jobs and wives. "Do you mind that he saw us?" she blurted.

"It ain't my union. I'm maintenance." His hand was on her hip. "So far as Hazel knows, we're still working on your house."

He stood so easily, with his hand resting on her, it was as though her body were long familiar to him. "I'll drive you home after work."

She nodded her head.

"What happened to your eye?"

"I tripped last night on Alling Street."

"You want to put a tea bag on it."

He was gone; she listened to his boots on the stairs, clomping through the halls.

She walked to her class.

They were standing around, smoking, talking to each other. She sat down at her chair in front and watched them for a while, then cleared her throat. "You're dismissed."

Some of them left, and some ignored her.

She went down the stairs and out.

The afternoon was gray, with autumn rustling through

the trees, tossing russet leaves on the pathway, where she walked, head down, through the gates, into town.

She entered Swizer's Drug Store.

"Can I help you, Miss deVos?"

Beside the sanitary napkins was a lineup of creams and foams; she chose a kit in a green carton.

"That's five twenty-five, please."

She placed the package in her handbag. She'd had a diaphragm for Clem, but when she came across it several years ago, it had crumbled in her hands.

She started back to the campus with her contraceptive kit and a surfeit of media knowledge about spermicidals, pills, coils, condoms . . . condoms decreased a man's sensitivity.

She paused in the middle of Woodward Street. A man's sensitivity.

Cars screeched their brakes. She darted to the sidewalk. How could she make it through the rest of the day?

She took the long way back to her office, past the fine arts building, where she knew he was working now.

He leaned on his shovel as she passed, and smiled up at her, his gap-toothed foolish smile.

She walked past him, turning down the road which led to the English building.

Wilson and Curdy were on the steps.

It was that other world again, the world of Associate Professor deVos. She took a deep breath. "Hello, Peter. Hello, Donald."

Wilson blocked her passage. "Leona, I was just asking after you. Did you have a good summer?"

"The usual. Poetry one-oh-nine. Beowulf to the brothers Anon."

He shook his head. "What ambition. We went to Spain for a change. One gets so sick of France."

"Has something been malfunctioning in your office?" asked Curdy. "Light bulbs or something?"

"Not that I know of."

"Odd. I thought I noticed one of the work crew . . ." He jangled some coins in his pocket. "What happened to your eye?"

"I took a fall on Alling Street."

Wilson gave his jovial laugh. "Isn't it rather early for ice, even on Alling Street?"

She clutched her handbag, waiting for them to let her pass, and realized she was holding it in front of her groin.

"You must come around and see us sometime," said Wilson. "Muriel would be delighted."

"Ditto," said Curdy.

She tried to maneuver around them. "And you must tell me about Spain sometime."

"It looks like I'm going to have several very promising students this term." Wilson took out a thin cigar and pierced it with a tool. "Are you planning to publish anything soon, Leona?"

"I don't know."

"You must be almost finished with your work on Donne." Curdy yawned, flapping his hand in front of his mouth.

"I have some work I must finish now." Her voice snapped like a whip, and they jumped away from the door.

She felt their eyes behind her, but by the time she reached her office, Professor deVos and her world were gone. She sat down at her desk, took out the package, unfolded the instruction sheet.

Shake well . . . invert . . . insert.

With Clem, she'd put in her diaphragm before going to their conferences, but the foam instruction sheet said apply before each intercourse. Suppose it turned him off to see her do it?

The four o'clock bell rang.

She stood at her window, watching the students stream

165

out of brick buildings. She felt the mass of their adolescent eros swarm up to where she stood, and it was just a tickle compared to her own desire.

She opened the sash, listening to their voices, cars starting up, friends calling their good-byes, each sound bringing her closer to four-thirty.

She went to the ladies' room, washed, and ran a comb through her hair.

He was at the parking lot before she was, leaning up against the Bluebird, a big man, wearing a rough plaid shirt, patched work pants and a dark green knitted cap.

He touched her hand, opened the door for her and walked around to the other side.

The Bluebird started up at once.

"Don't sit so far," he said.

She moved as close as she could.

He put his arm around her waist, bringing up long-buried dreams of going out on dates, driving with a boy, going steady, movies, soda fountains. Her arm was in the way.

They rode in silence down Sussex Avenue, Alling, Farrier Lane.

They walked together up the path, and she fumbled with the lock.

They stood inside the shack, looking at each other.

"I bought . . ." She opened her handbag. "I hope it doesn't bother you." She laid the package on the table.

He picked it up and read the label, taking a package out of his pocket. "I bought a box of jeezly rubbers." He tossed them on the table.

"Whichever you want . . . I don't know . . . I read . . ."

He pulled her to him and kissed her on the lips.

It was a tender, close-mouthed kiss, which ended with them once again staring, less sure of their movements than ever, so far was that soft surprising kiss from the practical

166

problem of foam versus rubbers.

He put his hand to her jacket, avoiding breasts and buttons, as though his hand were a wand that could wish the garment off, "I'll do it," she said, and quickly unfastened her clothes, without turning away, afraid he'd disappear, until her tweed suit lay heaped around her, and her blouse, and she stood like a grounded flamingo in pink knit vest and knee-length woollies, and all the time he too was taking off his clothes, without breaking the bright blue ring of his gaze which held her encircled.

"I could turn off the light," he said.

"Would you rather?"

He was down to his shorts, and she had stopped at her vest and woollies. "If it'd make you easier," he said.

"I don't mind."

He touched the ribbon which rimmed her vest, and pushed it slowly off her shoulder. His rough hand lay light on her skin, then swept aside the fabric covering the other breast. A shudder rippled her flesh.

She unsnapped his shorts. "Been growing all day," he laughed, half apologetically.

He stepped from his tangle of clothes, and came close. She felt the warmth of his breath, the tips of her nipples just touching his chest; with an exquisite shock their desire met. She sighed, and leaned into it.

His lips were warm and accepting, his calloused hands delicate as feathers, feathering down her sides and thighs, fitting themselves to the slope of her buttocks.

Her hips swayed, guided by his hands, and the shock of delight grew more intense.

She was aware that they were walking, that he was edging her toward the bed, that the dam within her had burst and bathed over them both and was sweeping them forward in a stream of longing as old as she was.

As they sank to the cot, she glimpsed her foam and his

condoms on the table, and then the fleeting image was gone, swept away like rubbers you see floating by on the river.

His lips searched hers; her answer was urgent. She reveled in her need. Nine years . . . How could I have gone so long? It's a wonder I didn't rape the janitor. . . . But I am raping the janitor. Soft kisses were pressed to her breast, and in the rush of her pleasure, she felt his tenderness. She hadn't waited nine years, she realized. She'd waited all her life.

His kisses got rougher, and her rush of pleasure became a surge. Something tremendous was opening, she was coming apart, she'd made a mistake. . . . With a great sigh, she relaxed.

The exact shape of his desire joined hers in a rhythmic searching. Perhaps after all, she thought, it wasn't a very bad thing that she was such a long stretch, and really she felt rather glad that there was so much of her to satisfy this big man with the odor of pine and hard knots of muscle and the girth of a tree trunk.

He slid his hands beneath her and moved her. She hadn't been aware that their position was imperfect, that they'd fallen to the bed at an angle, until she was lifted like a sheet of paper. And the shock of his physical strength was another in the many streams of pleasure that were surging through her; how could she possibly seem big and clumsy to someone who could lift her so easily?

He held nothing back from his offering; maybe he knew no other way. There was no part of him elsewhere, aloof or indifferent; the force of his surrender overwhelmed her. And gradually, she couldn't distinguish anything anymore but the turn of his warmth . . . the creaking of the cot . . . and the fine, shimmering curve of her rapture.

"Fancy you going in the same day as me."

Being as it was just the two of them at the bus stop, Hazel felt she had to say something.

"I been intending to do some Christmas shopping all week," said June.

Hazel straightened her wig. "Mine's more of a spur-of-the-minute trip."

The wind blew against them, and they backed away from the highway, sheltering under the trees.

"I hear the stores are terrible."

"I hear it too." Hazel was wearing her new pile coat and pile-lined boots.

"There it is." June ran out into the road, flagging the bus with her handbag.

"All the way, girls?"

"All the way."

They paid their fares and walked toward the back.

June sat down beside the window.

Hazel wasn't quite sure. She didn't want to appear stand-offish. "Do you mind?"

"Plenty of room." June moved farther toward the window to show Hazel she meant it, patting the place beside her.

"No point in sitting alone."

"Course not."

They arranged their coats and skirts and legs.

"Cold out today."

"Vicious."

"No weather for hanging a wash."

Hazel looked past June, out the window at the washlines stiff with frozen clothing. "Did you get your dryer yet?"

"I expect I'll get it Christmas morning."

"Makes quite a difference, it does."

"Oh, you got one, did you?"

"A while ago." The cows was in the barn at Patterson's farm, and both brick chimneys was going on the big old house. "Pattersons use thirty cord a winter."

"I heard twenty-six."

"Bliss cut for them one year."

"I guess he'd know then," June admitted. "How is Bliss these days?"

"Getting along. He's still remodeling Miss deVos's house."

"You wouldn't think there'd be that much work."

"She's terrible fussy about everything. A person can't just slap together a couple of boards for Miss deVos."

"He's lucky though, ain't he. Jobs are awful scarce this winter."

"Scarce for them that doesn't want to work."

"That's the truth," said June. "All them Hennessy boys on welfare. There's not a one of them couldn't find some honest employment if they had a mind to."

"It's just us few that work as is supporting the rest of the country."

"It can't go on forever, that's what Avery says."

"How is Avery?"

"Not too bad."

"And Donny?"

"Growing."

"That's nice."

"You ought to come over and take a look sometime."

Hazel picked a piece of lint off her skirt. "You ought to drop by and take a look at Joey."

"Yes, I might."

"And have a donut."

"I might come by this week."

"I suppose you're quite busy with them card parties."

"Only Thursdays," said June.

Hazel looked out the window at the trailers of Temperance Hollow. Not going to card parties was the main hitch in being Pentecostal.

June tapped the window. "There she is, herself."

Hazel peered out, but all she caught was a glimpse of the shack door closing behind Shyola's back. "Was she standing in the road?"

"Taking her chamber to the outhouse."

"More likely his chamber."

"More likely."

"How'd she look?"

"I couldn't see her all that good."

"She used to be real pretty." Hazel scratched herself inside her coat. It give her an odd turn to think of her school friend laying underneath some wrinkled old codger. She scratched herself again. Bliss was feeling so tired lately.

"O'Hara's house."

Hazel sat up to attention. "New curtains."

"Naturally. If we was on welfare, we'd have new curtains too."

"You might say we bought them curtains for them."

"How's that?" asked June.

"Us paying the taxes that bought them."

"I never thought of it so personal as O'Hara's curtains."

They bounced along the Shannon Road.

"All them shacks," said Hazel.

"Curtains into every one of them."

They crossed the bridge; the two women pulled on their gloves.

"Where you going first?" asked Hazel.

"Zeller's."

Hazel checked her wig in her mirror.

"Where you going first?" asked June.

"Zeller's."

They stopped at the terminal.

"Sure is cold."

"Don't them Christmas lights look nice?" Hazel walked beside her neighbor. "I always think Front Street looks like a picture with them lights."

"I got to run in the bank," said June. "I'll only be a minute."

"I'll go with you." Hazel sat down in a chair not too far from money orders.

The bank was seething with people. She glanced behind the counter. Not there.

She smoothed her coat and put on a pleasant face. He might be roaming among the crowd.

There was that box for the Orphans' Christmas. She opened her handbag, and took out two nickels. Maybe he was on his coffee break.

She waited with the nickels. It'd be a shame if she dropped them into the box and Tom Flagerty walked in after the fact.

"That's that," said June.

Hazel got to her feet.

"Ain't you coming, Hazel?"

"I'm just going to drop some money into the Orphans' Box."

"I guess I'll put some in too."

They walked back out to the street.

What a disappointing day! First she missed Shyola Dixon and now Tom Flagerty. She swiveled on the pavement.

"Who was that?" asked June.

"Tom Flagerty, works in money orders." He hadn't even seen her. If June hadn't been gabbing so much, she would've been looking ahead and they never would've missed each other. This was what she got from traveling with June Setzer.

They pushed into Zeller's.

"Land!"

"Did you ever see such a crowd?"

And such silver trees and angels and Elvis Presley singing "Silent Night" and coats and dresses and jewelry and perfume and a big sled filled with fancy wrappings and dishes and glasses and toys and skates and panty hose and lacy scarfs and radios and color TV sets and the loveliest wigs and shoes with sparkle and . . .

"I got to go up to infants'," said June.

"I'll be there in a bit," said Hazel. She walked slowly through the aisles, not even touching nothing, just listening to Elvis, and sniffing the colognes, and looking at all the beauty. Millions and billions and gillions of things, every one of them new and clean, laid out among the tinsel and the

Santas and the wreaths and the purple snowflakes twirling from the ceiling. An ordinary person, like June, with no religion that mattered, could never understand how Hazel felt about Christmas.

It was snowing lightly. She stopped for a moment, spreading her arms like a scarecrow, and raising her face to taste the cold delicious drops.

Her skin had grown fine beneath Bliss's calloused hands; she was all nerve endings, tuned to ecstasy.

She picked up her briefcase and continued up the path to the lot, loping along in her shapeless tweed coat and big galoshes.

The Bluebird's back was feathered white. She leaned across the hood, wiping the snow from the windshield.

An arm slid around her waist.

"Had trouble with my damn drill, or I would have got here sooner." His coarse yellow mitten fell away, and she followed him into the car, fitting her tweed angles somehow perfectly to his body, which was waiting white and impatient beneath layers of winter clothing.

He cocked his head to listen to the Bluebird's motor. It sparked, coughed, turned over.

"Another week I'll have to put my snow tires on." He took off his mittens and slipped his hand beneath her skirt, stroking her thighs, while she sat dizzily passive, glowing inside her woollies, with visions of security guards coming upon them. The department head had given her a peculiar look today; the gossip had gone beyond Wilson and Curdy; it would reach Bliss; he'd be frightened away.

His hand was gone, steering the Bluebird out of the lot.

They drove through the campus, headlights catching a few last students, a leafless tree, the steps of a building, coated with snow.

The houses on Sussex Avenue were lit for evening. She saw a woman setting her table beneath a crystal chandelier.

The car turned left on Alling Street, parked in Farrier Lane.

They entered the shack, and moved about in dusky shadows, she putting down her briefcase, he carefully hanging his jacket and cap. With a curious gallantry he helped her remove her galoshes, and the weight of those silly galoshes, which really couldn't have been very great, seemed tremendous; as he took them from her, she grew light.

In the corner of the room, the oil heater made a little putt-putt sound, and falling snowflakes laced the windowpanes. Lying on the cot, beneath his gentle weight, her mind searched out familiar burdens; but it seemed he'd taken them.

Like the night-blooming cereus she'd watched as a child, which after waiting so long to flower had become a bouquet in a single night, she felt her tightly furled petals open.

Snowflakes curtained the windows with fluttery veils.

Beneath her shelves of books, in the darkness, she read him like braille, and found his poetry more exquisite than any written—his shoulders broad, hips narrow, his foot arched the way it did and the back of his powerful neck curved inward ever so slightly.

The smell of him where she kissed the nape of his neck contrasted with the scent of his chest, the heady odor under his arms, the musk of his genitals, the hundred perfumes of her intoxication.

The muscles of his arms and chest, like supple, polished wood, and the soft fold where thigh met buttock, the harsh hair of his legs, the velvets and satins and crags, all were to be savored and served, and he returned each caress, showing her trembling flesh that what she'd learned from Clem was only half.

In recalling what Clem taught her, she did some things which made Bliss sit up and laugh.

"Come back here, Leona." He scooped her in his arms. "That feller must have thought you was a puppy dog."

She nestled beside him on the pillow.

"Tell me something," he demanded.

She whispered in his ear.

"I heard it a dozen times." He gave her a pinch on the rear. "Just talk to me."

She talked to him. She described the yellow light her childhood room wore in the evening; she told him about her brother down the hall and her mother and her father, all of them so far apart, and about the musty books and the taste of sea biscuits spread with apple jelly. "The evenings were so long," she said softly, "and now they're so short."

At the thought of how short the evenings were, they came together again.

And then they had to separate.

She helped him into his clothes, planting kisses on his skin, which was moist with her sweat. She knelt with his shorts, and he stepped into them, resting his hand on her shoulder. His lean, hard body grew bulkier and bulkier in undershirt, thermal shirt, thick thermal long johns, flannel work shirt, scratchy winter slacks and a grease-stained quilted vest. He sat on the cot while she laced his cumbersome boots, smeared with sweet-smelling coconut oil.

"Well, Miss deVos"—he took out his tobacco—"we got quite a bit of work done on the house tonight."

She sat naked on the floor, between his baggy legs, watching him roll a cigarette.

"Course," he said, "I ain't a professional carpenter, more of an odd job man."

She inhaled the aroma of his tobacco like an addict.

He struck a match and held it up to her face. "Miss deVos, you look happy as a pig in shit." He lit his cigarette. "And I figure I look about the same."

Janie landed on the bed with a thud.

"Go away."

"Mommy, I think Joey's hungry."

"You think yourself back to bed."

"Daddy, are you awake?"

"Eh? What is it, Janie?"

"It's Christmas."

"Christmas!" He rubbed his eyes. "I didn't hear nothing in the night. Sure hope the old feller didn't forget us."

"Look under the tree, Daddy. It's polluted with presents!"

"It appears the old feller made it."

"A person may as well try to sleep in Zeller's as in this house!"

"It's almost light, Mommy."

"Guess we better get up." Bliss swung his legs over the bed, and Hazel came grumbling after.

"Can we open them now?"

"Breakfast first."

"We stretch it out that way, see," Bliss explained.

Hazel headed for the bathroom. Tired? That wasn't the word! Up half the night wrapping presents, her at one end of the room, Bliss at the other, then together getting Janie's ready, and all the baby things for Joey. She washed her face, and tied on her terry robe.

Bliss came into the bathroom as she left.

"I started breakfast, Mommy," said Janie.

"Keep your hands off them cranberries."

"I wonder what I got!" Janie jumped around the table. "I seen a package that looked like a toboggan."

"Yes, and it's for Joey."

"A baby toboggan! Won't we look cute, me pulling him over the roads."

"He ain't to go in the roads."

"He's up!"

"May as well feed him." Hazel went into the children's room and changed the baby, then carried him into the kitchen and set him in his highchair, stopping to switch on the TV.

Bliss had poured the coffee.

Janie banged with her spoon. " 'Rudolph the red-nosed reindeer, Had a very shiny nose! And if you ever saw him, You would even say it glows'!"

"Have some toast, Hazel."

She spooned on marmalade. "I was hoping the family might come by after dinner to look at the presents, but it don't look like a day for traveling." Showing her presents to the family was one of the things about Christmas. Not that she lorded it, but she did get a lot, more-so than any of the others.

"It's snowing hard," said Bliss.

"I'm finished," announced Janie.

"Then you can feed your brother." Hazel chewed her toast.

"Here, Joey."

Bliss ate the last of his Sugar Crisps. "If it keeps on snowing, some folks might get to pull a new toboggan."

"Joey don't want no more."

"Okay." Bliss stood. "Who's going to open first?"

Hazel pointed to a square parcel under the tree. "Open that one first, Janie."

She tore the wrapping off. "Oh, Mommy, it's a Wee Lady manicure kit! Look, Daddy."

"Ain't that pretty."

Bliss picked up a red-wrapped package and carried it to his wife.

Hazel put down her coffee. "Now Bliss, that's just what I wanted!" She always gave him a list, but still it was a surprise to see he got it right. She held up the white blouse. It was even nicer than the one she seen in K-Mart, more frills onto it. "Wash 'n' wear too." She folded it back in the box, leaving the lid off for show. "You open one for Joey."

Janie ripped the paper off the toboggan.

"What about me?" asked Bliss.

"Give your father that blue box there."

Bliss put the package to his ear and shook it, held it up to the light, turned it around. "I wonder what could be in here." He took off the wrapping slowly. "What do you think it is, Janie?"

"I ain't telling."

"Well, look at that! New socks."

"My turn!" Janie stripped another package. "Ooooooooh, a wristwatch!"

"Give it here, I'll set it for you." Bliss strapped it on his daughter's wrist.

"Your turn, Mommy."

"Give me that there speckled one."

"I bet I know what it is."

"I bet you do too." Hazel took off the paper. "Now we can eat some candy while we open the rest of them."

"Joey's turn." Janie took the wrapping off a blue furry snowsuit.

"Give your father the one you got him."

"Here, Daddy."

Bliss went through his ritual, shaking it, holding it up to the light, untying the ribbon slowly. "Makings! I'm going to light me up a cigarette right now." He shook the new tobacco into the new paper and rolled it between his fingers.

"Here I go," sang Janie, tearing apart another parcel. "Oh boys, oh days, I'll look pretty in this!"

"Give your mother that big one in the corner."

"Well now, my new robe." Hazel changed from the old one, and did a few turns, looking at herself in the mirror.

"I couldn't find no mauve one like you asked for," Bliss apologized.

"This one's perfect." Pink really was her color.

Janie ripped open Joey's packages.

Wrapping paper covered the floor.

"Ain't this sweet."

"A feller's set for socks for the rest of the winter."

"Exactly what I wanted."

Hazel eyed the window from time to time. They'd never get through today. The roads might open tomorrow, but tomorrow she wanted to go and pay some calls herself.

"Oh no," wailed Janie. "That's everything."

"There's one more," said Hazel.

"That's right." Janie put her hand in front of her mouth. "Wait till you see it, Daddy!"

"Something more for me?" Bliss was jiggling Joey on his knee. "I think I did pretty good."

"Just you wait one minute." Hazel swished into the kids' room, in her new bathrobe.

She pulled away the laundry basket and the towels she'd thrown over it.

"Here it comes!" shouted Janie.

Bliss looked up from Joey.

Hazel wheeled it in front of him. "Merry Christmas, Bliss."

"Ain't it beautiful, Daddy!"

"Jesus Christ."

Hazel thought she'd ignore the language, even though it was His own day. "You're pleased, ain't you?"

"How much did it cost?"

"Don't you know you ain't supposed to ask how much presents cost." She pushed it closer to him. "See this here knob? Auto-Chroma Purity Control."

"Where'd you get it, Hazel?"

"Down to Easy Credit Electric."

"With what?"

"I signed a paper. They was real nice about it. I explained how it was a surprise, and they looked us up and said we got excellent standing."

"It's a color TV, Daddy!"

"I can see that, Janie."

"Ain't we going to plug it in?"

Bliss lowered Joey into his playpen, and unplugged the other television. "Where do you want this one?"

"In my room. Ain't that right, Mommy?"

He carried the black-and-white set into the other room.

"Boys, I can't wait, huh, Mommy. Is Sesame Street on today?"

"I don't think it," said Hazel. There'd been one bad minute, when he first caught sight of it, but everything would be all right now. She ran her hand over the shiny cabinet.

"Was there any special instructions come with it?"

She handed him the papers and walked to the window. If this snow kept up, and the family couldn't get through to see what Bliss got her for Christmas, it would be a terrible shame. It was always such a treat for them to admire her stuff, and this year it would be even more-so, in Auto-Chroma Purity Color.

She stood at her office window, watching a man on a ladder chopping ice off the roof of the psychology building across the way. His collar was up, his knit cap pulled down over his ears, and the ladder swayed slightly in the wind.

It was inter-session, and the grades were in. She had no more papers to mark. She no longer worked on her book. She had no reason to come to school. But the man across the way . . .

For a second, he became a stranger, and she couldn't stand it, to be outside his life, to have nothing to do with him.

She flung on her coat and went downstairs.

He was climbing down the ladder backward.

"Where are you going now?" she asked.

"To the biology building."

He held his ax under one arm, the ladder under the other. Walking with him on campus, where they couldn't touch, was an irresistible torture she inflicted on herself. And on him too—she could sense his desire stirring, could smell it in the wind which bit her face and fingers; she'd forgotten her gloves in the rush.

They stopped in front of the biology building.

"Bliss?"

"Eh?"

"I was watching you chop the ice and I wanted you so much, but it was as though you were unattainable, as though it wasn't you, and after I realized it was you . . ." She saw she was talking nonsense. "You looked nice," she added lamely.

He looked down at her hands. "You're going to get frostbite."

She put her hands in her pockets.

"I'll see you in an hour." He turned away from her, setting the ladder up against the wall.

She walked back to the English building. Underneath her pink woolen undershirt, between her breasts, was a tiny gold locket he'd given her for Christmas.

She climbed the stairs and entered her office. The travel posters of the thatch-roofed cottages where she used to live in her imagination with Shakespeare and Herrick were no longer on the wall. She no longer yearned for another time, an enchanted land, a lofty romance.

At four-thirty, she went to the Bluebird; he arrived at the same time.

The motor stalled, finally started. They waited for it to warm, their bodies glued at the thigh like Siamese twins.

"Some snow backed up through one of them patent shingles and leaked into a dean's office."

Dean Chiasson had summoned her to his office before inter-session. She'd gone with a sense of doom, sure it involved Bliss, but it was only about the poetry contest.

They wound their way down the hill, out onto Sussex Avenue. Some few Christmas decorations still twinkled around doorways and flashed red and blue on spruce trees in the yards.

On Alling Street, a single house kept up the celebration.

In Farrier Lane, the oil stove cast a faint aura through the windows of her shack.

He made a fire in the Franklin, in front of which lay a new shag rug, where they knelt, and took off each other's clothes. For her the flames were a candelabrum, lighting the marvelous feast of Bliss's body. How her own body looked in the fire's glow she didn't care to know; all that mattered was his pale eyes shining on her like a mirror, reflecting not her hateful homeliness, but her love.

His calloused fingers played her skin like the strings of a guitar, plucking forth melodies of loveliness and torment, repeating the same tantalizing notes over and over like a drone. Her organs reverberated, harmonies rising and falling, welling and spreading out until she was diffused, scattered like broken chords, exposed and open on the carpet.

She twined her long legs around him, and felt him penetrating her nature, probing her loneliest secrets with delicate friction. The rough hair of his thighs brushed against her as they rocked; her breasts in his hands were little animals, quivering to an impossible climax of their own.

And when she came, surging with him, layer after layer, it was like a great unfolding of happiness and sorrow, as though all her life and his were mixed and flowing, freeing them from past and future in this ecstasy of flesh.

He slept, and she kept watch.

The fire flickered on his face, every flaw of which she knew, but whose beauty still amazed her. She traced the arteries of his neck and the swollen veins of his arms, the complex capillaries of his genitals. As his chest rose and fell, she envisioned his blood pumping through the fragile network of his body, a system that could be annihilated in an instant. She understood mortality, and in the fear that clutched her, their encounter moved her as an infinitely sad and fleeting thing.

Somewhere beyond the wall, she heard the scurrying of mice.

His body twitched on the rug; he emitted a low grunt.

How funny he was, licking his lips in his sleep.

She studied his face, then tilted her head and looked from another angle. She looked at him upside down. She bent over him quietly, and pressed his ears against his head.

He opened his eyes. "Think they spoil my beauty, do you?"

She took her hands away, letting the ears flap out. "They enhance your beauty."

He reached for his paper and tobacco. "You shouldn't let me sleep."

"I always wake you in time."

"It ain't that. It's us losing the minutes." He rolled a cigarette and lit it.

"You were licking your lips."

He grinned. "I was dreaming of something I'm going to do to you."

She touched her finger to his navel.

"Don't rush a feller."

"You won't forget?"

"Not likely." He laughed on his smoke, choking and spluttering.

"I worry about your health."

"Coughing's good for a person."

"I never heard that before."

"Lots of things you city slickers never heard." He flicked his ash on the ledge of the stove. "What will you do all weekend?"

"Look forward to Monday."

"That's about the size of it."

"I'm not complaining."

"I know you ain't." He watched his smoke rise. "Maybe I am."

She was silent.

"I guess I'm a greedy bastard." He stubbed his cigarette, and dropped it behind the screen.

"I'm greedy too," she said, trailing her hand down his belly.

He lay back on the rug. "That's why I'm partial to you."

"Have another donut."

"Don't mind if I do," said June.

"I shouldn't have any myself." Hazel dunked one in her tea. "Getting so fat as I am."

"A person has to eat."

The women didn't face each other but faced the TV, where Young Tony Andrews was cheating on Emmeline in color.

Beside the TV set, Joey and Donny stared at each other in the playpen.

"I wonder," said June, "if the day will ever be that they don't make no more black and white."

"Don't you feel bad, June." Hazel poured her guest more tea. "Your turn will come too. I have a feeling."

"I ain't so sure. I been after Avery since Christmas to get himself an evening job, but he says there ain't none to be had."

"Did you send him over to Manpower?"

"He been there two or three times."

"You got to keep right after them people at Manpower, so as they know you mean business."

"I don't know why Young Tony Andrews took up with this one."

Hazel looked at the face on the screen. "I guess some men just favor the slutty type." She really hadn't ought to have said that, considering June.

"Speaking of slutty types," said June, "did you hear about Mary Inch?"

"I don't know if I heard the same as you did. The story I got was her old man turned her out."

"She was wandering the streets for three days before someone give her a room."

"What I can't understand is why he waited so long."

"He was waiting till the mortgage was paid, see. It come out of Mary's inheritance."

"You mean he was putting up with her roving all them years, waiting on the mortgage?"

June helped herself to another donut. "Old Inch was always a deep thinker."

"I guess she ain't got none of it left, if she had to wander the streets."

"It all went into the house."

"Have you ever been into it?"

"I ain't," said June, "but Stella has. Glass-front china cupboard, color TV, lamps on every table."

"All from Mary's inheritance?"

"That's what they say."

Hazel sipped thoughtfully. "There was Inch all them years, letting everyone think him a fool, and him just biding his time."

"I feel kind of sorry for Mary."

"She can always get back her job washing dishes down to the Ambassador."

"Hard for a woman her age, standing on her feet all day."

"Her with the varicose too."

"You think the children might have helped her out, but they shut their doors in her face."

"Probably afraid old Inch would cut them off."

"He would."

"They're a long-headed bunch all right."

"Not Mary."

"No, she didn't work it so smart."

"I hear tell he never voiced a word, not once in forty years, to give her the hint he minded."

"She could have suspected though. Most men mind."

"That ain't quite true," said June.

Hazel took another donut. She couldn't very well argue with June over a thing like that. Wouldn't it be something though, if forty years from now, Avery turned June out in the road?

There was a knock on the door.

"I wonder who that would be."

"Might be Mabel."

"Not at this hour."

"Jehovah's Witnesses, likely."

There was another knock.

"I suppose you ought to find out."

"Could be the Fuller Brush." Hazel got up and opened the door.

"Mrs. Bliss Dawson?"

"The same."

The man turned and called to another one, sitting in a truck. "This is the place."

"I didn't order nothing," said Hazel.

The two men came into the room, and looked around. "There she is, Hank."

Hank walked to the TV set, and yanked the plug from the wall. Young Tony Andrews dimmed and disappeared.

"Now just one minute!"

"Got the papers right here, ma'am. Wheel her to the door, Hank."

"Did you miss your payment, Hazel?" June stood up with her donut.

"Course not. Bliss makes all the payments." Hazel felt like she had to tumble over in a chair, but she held on to the edge of the table. "You bring that back this minute!"

"Here's the papers, ma'am. Mrs. Bliss Dawson, Fingabog Siding."

"Must be another Fingabog Siding."

Joey and Donny were standing up, staring over the top of the playpen.

"This is the set, all right."

"Call the store," suggested June.

"We'll wait, ma'am, if you want to call the store."

"Give me that piece of paper." Hazel rang for the operator. "Get me Easy Credit Electric." She tapped her foot. "It's an emergency."

"Ask to talk to Mr. Fielding."

"I want to talk to Mr. Fielding. Emergency." She heaved into the phone. These stores had too much business, couldn't keep their own records straight. "Mr. Fielding? This is Mrs. Bliss Dawson. Fingabog Siding. There's two men here trying to take my TV set." She turned to her visitors. "He's going to get his papers."

"You think they'd warn a person first," said June. "Anyone could forget a payment."

"Yes, that's right, Dawson. . . . He didn't? . . . Not January neither? . . . Yes. . . . Yes. . . ." She hung up. "Appears to be the same Fingabog Siding."

"Let's go, Hank."

"Excuse me, ma'am." The TV wheeled past her.

"I'm home!" Janie barged through the shed.

"Quit your hollering!"

"Where they taking our TV?"

"We'll leave this copy of the papers with you, ma'am." The door closed behind them.

"Did the color TV break, Mommy?"

"That's right," said June. "Listen, Hazel, I have to be going. Avery will be home for his supper soon."

"I can't figure what happened. Bliss always makes all our payments."

"Probably with so many different ones, this one just dodged his mind."

"Couldn't have nothing to do with money."

"Didn't we pay for the TV, Mommy?"

"After all, June, he makes good money down to the college, plus three dollar an hour at Miss deVos's."

"Like I said, it just dodged him."

"It ain't like Bliss though, to let a payment dodge him."

"Is that why they took our TV, cause Daddy dodged the payments?"

"I think I'll give you a ring, Hazel, later in the evening, to see how you're feeling. . . . Come on, Donny."

"So long, June." Hazel sat down in her rocker.

"We can watch Sesame Street on my set. Want me to bring it in?"

"It's too heavy for you to carry." They went into the children's room, and Hazel unplugged Janie's TV.

"Did we get poor, Mommy?"

194

"Course not." She plugged the old set in its place and turned it on to Camilla Starr.

"Can't we watch Sesame Street?"

"You be good, or I'll clobber you."

Janie sat down on the rug, and put her hand in her mother's lap. "If we're poor, will I have to go out to work like Daddy did when he was little?"

"We ain't poor."

"I wouldn't mind carrying grub out to the men in the woods. I could pull it on Joey's toboggan."

Hazel shook the hand off her lap, and got to her feet. "I can't mind the story with you yapping. You may as well turn on Sesame Street."

Janie switched the channel.

Hazel poured herself more tea, and sat down to a think and donut.

"A B C D E," sang Janie.

She hurried back to her office after eleven o'clock class, for every day at noon Bliss showed up with his lunch pail.

She put her briefcase in the corner, and plugged in the coffee pot.

He was late. That gave her time to comb her hair and collect herself. At the sound of his boots on the stairs her composure vanished.

He opened the door and pulled her against him, but his kiss was distracted.

She gently withdrew from his arms. "What's the matter?"

"Ain't nothing terrible."

196

"Are you sure?"

He locked the door. "Can you loan me sixty dollars?"

"Of course." She went for her purse. "Is that all you were worried about?"

"They took the old woman's TV set."

"They took it?"

"I never made any payments, see." He stuffed the money in his pocket. "I'll pay you as soon as I can."

"Whatever for?"

"I will, that's all." He sat back in his chair, and took out tobacco and paper. "Boys, the shit hit the fan. What am I doing with my money! Working every night to Miss deVos's, and can't even pay for a jeezly TV set."

"Why didn't you tell me!" She rummaged in her handbag, finally dumped it out on the desk. "Here." She handed him her bankbook.

"I don't want to see your bankbook."

"I want you to have it. Not the book, the money, whatever you'll take. I should've been paying you all these months when we . . . when you were supposed to be working."

"Shut up, Leona."

"I know I didn't phrase it right." She looked at the bankbook in her hands. "What I mean is it doesn't matter to me."

"Nor to me." He rolled his cigarette, spilling tobacco on the floor. "I wish I never mentioned the damn TV."

"If it weren't for me, they wouldn't have taken Hazel's television. You'd be earning enough to pay for it."

"That ain't true. Jobs are scarce in winter."

"At least let me pay for the television."

"Sixty dollars will bring it back."

"What about the rest of the payments?"

"I'll worry about them when the time comes."

"I earn five times as much as I spend."

"Your coffee's boiled away."

She got up and unplugged the pot.

He was writing on a slip of paper, *I.O.U. $60. Bliss.*

"Why can't you take my money, as a friend?"

"Cause we ain't friends."

The doorknob rattled. There was a knock on the door. Bliss leaned over and turned the latch.

"Sorry to always intrude." Curdy sat down on the metal cabinet.

"Did you want to borrow something, Donald?"

"Strictly a social visit." He looked around, at Bliss, at the desk, which was jumbled with the contents of Leona's pocketbook, at the I.O.U. "We rarely see you any more."

"I have a heavy work load this term."

"So I see." He glanced again at Bliss, who was smoking his cigarette and gazing out the window.

"It was nice of you to stop by, Donald. Come again sometime."

"I did have something to tell you. I was wondering whether you saw the notice on the board about Clem Stegmann speaking here next month."

"Yes, I saw it."

"I'm throwing a party afterwards. Just a small group of people who'd really be interested. I remember that you studied with him once."

"I did my thesis with him."

"So you'll be there. Good. Well, I won't keep you two any longer from your lunch."

Bliss locked the door. "Nosy parker, ain't he. Probably puts a glass to the wall so he can listen better."

"Curdy's not as bad as all that."

He took out his sandwiches. "Where's your lunch?"

She opened her briefcase.

"Are you going to his party?"

"No."

"There ain't nothing there to interest you?"

"No."

He chomped on his sandwich. "Would you have gone to his party if . . ."

"If I hadn't met you? Yes." She put out her hand and touched him on the sleeve. "Don't you know yet how things are? I wouldn't care if Clem Stegmann strewed my bed with flowers."

"Eat your lunch."

She unwrapped her sandwich.

"Did he throw flowers on your bed?"

"He told me about it."

"I never thought to buy you flowers."

"I'd be furious if you did, now that I know how pressed you are for money."

"When spring comes, I'll pick you mayflowers."

"I'd rather you spent the time with me than picking mayflowers."

"Take some of my tea. There's enough."

She drank tea from his thermos mug.

He finished his sandwich. "I got to take the money over to Easy Credit."

"Can I go with you?"

"Better not. There's so many people a feller is liable to run into in town."

"I've made things hard for you in a lot of ways, haven't I."

He laughed. "You're a real hardship, you are. That's why I can't hardly wait to see you every day." He closed his lunch pail and stood. "You can walk me to the car."

They clattered down the stairs, and made their way up the path, through the bustle of students.

"You said jobs are scarce in winter. I guess when summer comes, there'll be other work for you."

"I found the work I want."

"I'll have to start paying you three dollars an hour."

"Think I'm worth three dollars, do you?"

She smiled. "I read somewhere that prostitutes charge for each orgasm."

"I'd have you cleaned out in a week."

"You're going to be a real good player soon," said June. "You can see for yourself lots of them girls been coming to card parties for years didn't do as good as you did today."

"I do seem to have the knack," agreed Hazel. It wasn't as though she'd lowered her standard; the way she explained it to Bliss was now that she seen there wasn't no money gambling—just little do-hick prizes like salt and pepper shakers or a quart of pop—it would be plain stubbornness for her to stay away from a simple pleasure.

Lord knows she had little enough pleasure.

"Coming in for tea?" asked June.

"I guess."

"You seem a bit under the weather."

"Only a case of spring fever."

"It ain't even the middle of March," said June.

Hazel followed her into the house. The fact of the act was, though she'd never admit it to her neighbor, two jobs was too much for any man. It tuckered him clear useless.

"Have a seat," said June. "I'm going to run over to Mrs. Ives's house for Donny."

Hazel switched on June's TV. There was Emmeline in black and white. It was the thought of having her own color TV whipped away again from under her nose that kept her from suggesting Bliss quit working evenings. Every cloud had its lining, they said, and they might as well say every lining come with its cloud. She sat down in front of the story.

"What's up?" June was back with Donny.

"That Emmeline sure needs a pair of glasses. She wouldn't see her own nose if it wasn't tacked to her face."

"The one who should is always the last to know."

Hazel wondered whether Avery was the last to know about June.

"Tea'll be ready in a minute." June got the fire going, and pushed the kettle to the front of the stove.

"You know that feller Carol Bidlake's running around with?"

"I never seen him but through the car."

"I hear tell she ain't the first married girl he's had his eye to."

"Who else has he had his eye to?"

"Different ones, they say." Hazel tugged at a hangnail. "Celia Parkson's uncle who lives down Epsom Valley got it from his dentist."

"Come and have your tea now." June piled the platter with cookies.

"Marbleized. Nice."

"They're a refrigerator cookie."

Hazel crunched. "Did you see Theresa a-flukin' by last night?"

"I was sleeping, but I heard about it from Mrs. Ives."

"That girl will catch her death."

"If she don't catch something better."

"Tits flying in every direction."

"Where'd she land this time?"

"To Mabel's."

"So you must have seen her pretty good."

"Good enough. She went back home this morning wearing Mabel's raincoat."

"Two tempers in a house is one too much."

"I guess she broke the chairs and he broke half the dishes before she hit the road in her underpants."

"I wonder why it takes her like that."

"Temper."

"But other people have a row, they don't strip down before hauling out."

"She must get into a sweat is the only way I can figure it."

"Which ones was she wearing?"

"Plain black."

"I seen her once in a pair that said the day of the week onto it."

"Wednesday," Hazel nodded. "I seen her that time too."

"She has got a lovely shape."

Hazel sipped her tea. "You can't say nothing against her shape."

"Now they'll have to buy new dishes."

"I seen real nice dishes up to the K-Mart. Went by the name of Jasmine."

"What was they like?"

"In between a pink, an orange and a yellow."

"Any flowers onto them?"

"No." Hazel looked out the window. "The kids are letting out. I better go home for Janie."

"Take your cookie with you."

"I'll talk to you later, June."

"Come back again."

Hazel couldn't cut through the yards cause of the fence, so she walked home over the road. Next vacation, Bliss would have to take it down.

"Hi, Mommy!" Janie jumped up from the steps. "I been waiting for hours."

"You just got out." Hazel unlocked the door. "I'm going to Mabel's to get your brother."

"Okay." Janie snapped on the color TV.

Hazel waded through the bushes to Mabel's house; the old woman was sitting at her treadle.

"How was Joey?"

"Some smart!"

Hazel pulled up a chair.

"You ain't looking your usual perky, Hazel."

Hazel sighed, kicking away a cat who was trying to climb on her lap. "I guess I'm just guinea-pooped."

"I still got raspberry vinegar left, if you think it would help you."

"I'll have a small taste."

Mabel felt her way to the pantry. "It should have some kick into it by now."

"You know I don't favor liquor."

"Only for a tonic." Mabel returned with a glassful.

"It is refreshing."

Camilla Starr was getting riled up over something, but Mabel's TV screen was more like sleet today.

"Theresa spent the night."

"I seen her running by."

"All that side of the family had an awful temper. My uncle that was Theresa's grandfather used to get into a rage and cut the tops off the begonias. One year he salted Aunt Jessie's bleeding heart."

"Did it die?"

"Course it died."

"Any of the others run bare-naked?"

"Theresa's the first."

Hazel finished the vinegar. "Thanks for taking care of Joey." She handed Mabel her dollar.

They went to the door, and Mabel called her cats.

"Kitty," called Joey.

"There!"

"Ain't he!"

"Like his father." Mabel patted the baby's head. "Bliss was always a smart bugger too."

Hazel lugged Joey home.

"If you want to watch Sesame Street, put it on in your own room!"

"I want to be with you and Joey."

"Then watch what we watch!" Hazel slammed the channels round to Camilla Starr.

"What's the matter, Mommy?"

"You."

"What did I do?"

"Just make sure you don't."

"Can I help you get supper?"

"You can peel the potatoes."

Janie took up the knife. "Want to hear a new song they taught us?"

"No."

" 'I know a friendly city, A happy place indeed, Where there are friendly people, Of every race and creed, And when a lonely stranger . . .' "

Hazel cuffed her on the head.

"You made me cut myself!"

"Let me see."

"Kiss it, Mommy."

"Come over to the sink and let me wash it."

"Ain't you going to kiss it?"

"Can't even trust you to peel potatoes. When I was seven, I was peeling potatoes and boiling them."

"Tell me about when you was seven."

"I got enough to do. Get your father to tell you them stories."

"You was boiling the potatoes and what else? Tell me, Mommy."

"Quit your pestering."

"Can I finish the potatoes?"

"If you're careful."

Janie took up the knife. " 'And when a lonely stranger, Walks down its friendly streets, He gets a friendly greeting . . . ' "

"Get!"

"What did I do?"

"I told you not to sing."

"I forgot."

"Get into your room."

"Stop pushing me, Mommy."

"And stay in until called." Hazel banged Janie's door shut. Kids. Kids. Kids.

"Kitty," said Joey from his playpen.

"You too!"

He stared at his toes.

Hazel sighed. Nothing on TV but news. She switched the channels. There was something.

"So hurry in to Lambert's Fashions, your first shop for career-girl clothes, where everything is now reduced by ten percent."

Hazel sat down in her rocker. Ten percent was a pretty good saving. The only trouble with Lambert's Fashions was they didn't carry size twenty.

"Stay in bed, Leona."

"Don't you want me to see you out?"

"I'm a little late."

She watched him dress through half-closed eyes, submitting to the luxury of drifting into sleep still awash with their last round of love.

He leaned over and kissed her eyes shut. "I'll let myself out."

The door closed behind him. It would be as if he'd never left if she could slip right into a dream:

He was coming toward her, floating across the campus, arms wide, smiling, and she floated out to meet him. Graceful as birds, they turned in the air, lightly falling through space, tumbling slowly downward, entwined, sailing downward . . .

A persistent knocking woke her.

She switched on the lamp by her bed. "You left it open."

He was fumbling with the knob.

"Bliss?"

The door swung to, followed by a breath of cold air, and cautiously, like a deep-sea diver moving through unknown waters, he entered the dimly lit shack. She pulled the blanket up over her breasts.

He stood in front of the door, getting his bearings. "I'm sorry I woke you. I tried to call first, but the operator said you had no phone."

Gray-bearded, slender, he stepped into the circle of light.

She wasn't sure if it was a dream . . . a murderer come to kill her . . . a thief . . . or someone she knew . . . and if so, who?

His face was familiar as her own.

Familiar also was her old sense of being ill at ease, too large, exposed, and somehow in need.

The room dissolved.

The years dissolved.

She was twenty, and the warmth of his smile promised something she'd been seeking all her life.

"Why don't you have a phone?" He walked over, and sat on the edge of her bed.

She laughed uncomfortably. "So you can call me every ten years?"

"You might have called too. Or written. Or stayed." He hadn't aged. Aside from the gray in his beard, he was remarkably the same. Probably from feeding on young flesh, she thought, and was immediately ashamed.

"How've you been, Clem?" she asked, attempting a worldliness she didn't feel.

"Looking forward to this trip. How have you been?"

"Very happy."

"You should be sad." The portion of cot between them narrowed as he crossed his legs; the gesture more than the words plunged her back.

"I'm being assaulted by memories."

"Assault's a poor choice of words. But, yes."

She smiled. "Did I ever say anything right?"

"As a matter of fact you did."

"What was it?"

"Something about me."

"I didn't think I had the nerve to say anything about you."

"You've forgotten, but I in my egomania haven't."

She had a suspicion she'd be a good deal more up to the situation if she weren't sitting in bed holding a blanket in front of her breasts . . . but that's the way it had always been with them, he fully clothed in his superiority and she undressed. "Do you still talk Latin to your students?"

"You were the only student to receive the benefit of my Latin." His attention, which had been riveted on her until this minute, seemed to draw back in. "May I mix myself a drink?"

"I'm afraid there's nothing."

He considered the information. "I suppose I've had enough."

"If you hand me my robe, I'll fix you something to eat."

"No."

"Did they feed you at the party?"

"No, I won't hand you your robe."

"Oh."

"Why didn't you come to the party? Weren't you even curious to see me?"

"I was busy." She met his hawk's gaze. "I have a friend."

"I heard."

"How did you hear?"

"It was the main topic of conversation. Leona deVos— dropping her drawers for the man who cleans the toilets."

She reddened. "You always had a way with words."

"Not my words. I'm quoting."

"It sounds like you."

"So that's how you remember me." His voice became less arrogant. "Was I always nasty?"

"Not always."

"Do you want to know how I remember you? As a shy gawky girl with whom I was a little in love for a long time."

She looked at his hands, which had taught her the little she knew of love before, and felt how much his words would have meant a year ago. "Now that it no longer matters . . ."

"I think it matters." He took out his pipe, then put it back, in a nervous gesture she didn't recall. "I'm fifty-three. That's a lot of years to look back on, and a lot of women, most of whom blend together."

"I'm thirty-five."

He studied her face, her shoulders, her fingers clutching the blanket. "Still shy. Still gawky. Still attractive to me."

"It's only the lighting, Clem."

"I feel protective toward you. Lust is purely secondary."

"What would you protect me against?"

"I understand he beats you. He sends you to school covered with bruises and black eyes."

"I was running on Alling Street and tripped."

"They say you support him and his family back in the hills. That he extorts gifts from you for his wife. A color television set."

"Don't tell me any more."

"How can you waste yourself on someone so far beneath you?"

"Did the gossip embarrass you?"

"Actually, it inspired me." He got up and went to the cupboard. "Don't you have anything at all to drink?"

"There's orange juice in the refrigerator."

He took it out. "Want some?"

"No thanks."

He came back to the bed, sat again on the edge; his mockery now seemed directed at himself. "Did you know I was a romantic?"

"No."

"Neither did I. But I must be. I feel like D'Artagnan come to save whatever-her-name-was."

"So you've come to save me?" She tried to keep from smiling.

"I'd like very much to save you."

She sensed something in his voice and was shocked to realize that he was lonely, had always been lonely.

He clasped his hands around his knee. "Let's start from the beginning. I've just walked in. Hello, Leona. What have you been doing with yourself?"

"Teaching."

"I read your book on Herrick."

"It was lousy, wasn't it."

"Thorough, but dry."

"I've dropped all that."

"They said you were doing a book on Donne."

She shook her head.

"Have you read my books?"

"I liked them."

"What a marvelously formal conversation. You're supposed to ask after my family next."

"How is your family?"

"Scattered to the four winds. I'm all alone."

"I'm sorry."

"I'd rather that you were glad."

"I'm glad if it's what you want."

"It's not what I want." He smiled, reaching out for her hand, and taking the blanket away instead.

The moment suspended.

She felt the ludicrousness of acting offended . . . felt that he saw the ludicrousness too, his own and hers, saw life as ludicrous, and it was this awareness which estranged him from everything.

They both heard the noise and turned at the same time.

Clem covered his head with his arms as the big man came toward him, but beneath his fear she knew he was laughing, would probably laugh if Bliss murdered him.

"Here, Leona." Bliss drew the blanket up around her. "You'll catch cold."

She wondered vaguely what it had been she'd found amusing a minute before.

"This is my teacher, Bliss."

"I know who it is." He dragged a chair over to the bed. The two men eyed each other, Bliss stolid, Clem amused.

"I suppose you've been out there a long time," he said.

"Yup."

Clem took out his pipe.

Bliss took out his cigarette paper. "I seen your car turn as I was leaving, so I figured I better come back. Nobody ever drives down Leona's lane but me."

Clem tamped the tobacco in his pipe. "Possessiveness. It comes from *possidere*, to hold, as opposed to *dominari*, to own absolutely."

Bliss rolled a cigarette. "Just passing through, are you?"

"I think I'll stay in town for the weekend."

"You planning to stay with one of them teachers?"

"She hasn't invited me yet."

Bliss turned to Leona.

"Of course I'm not going to invite him," she said, amazed that Bliss didn't know it, that he was as blind as Clem.

Clem lit his pipe. "I'm patient."

"You're just going to stick around?" asked Bliss.

"Frankly, I don't see that it's your concern."

"Leona's my lookout."

Clem took out a notebook and pen, murmuring to her, "I always jot down new colloquialisms."

"I want to know when you're planning to go, cause I got a family back in the hills like they said, and I can't watch over Leona's house on the weekend."

"That isn't very flattering to Leona."

"I don't have to flatter Leona. She knows how much I think of her." Bliss went into a fit of coughing.

"Rather strong blend you use."

"I guess we'll be setting here all night." Bliss leaned back in his chair, flicking his ash on the floor.

"Please go, Clem."

"If you wish. I didn't come to make things difficult for you. On the contrary." He stood. "Tomorrow then?"

"Not tomorrow neither," said Bliss.

Clem stirred the ashes in his pipe. "Leona has a right to her own decisions. Neither one of us has any claim on her."

"Suppose one of us was going to have?"

Clem frowned. "I'm not sure I understand."

"You understand."

Clem turned to her. "You aren't really going to marry him."

She gazed at Bliss and for an instant saw him through others' eyes—unsmiling, hard and ignorant. She turned to Clem and nodded.

He touched his finger to her cheek, then slowly took it away. "It seems you're no longer my lookout."

Bliss lumbered to his feet.

"No need to show me out," said Clem, straightening his shoulders. He put his hands in his pockets and walked jauntily to the door. "Since I'm obviously *de trop* at this party, I think I'll go back to the other."

Pausing at the door, he turned, and formed his fingers into a V.

They listened to him start his car and drive away.

"You don't mind, do you, Leona?" Bliss took Clem's place on the edge of her bed. "I mean that bit about getting married."

She shook her head.

"The way I figure it, a feller only lives once." He struggled through his smoke. "So he may as well live with the person who suits him."

She leaned her head on his lap and put her arms around his waist.

He stroked her back. "I bet that old cunt never scratched your back for you, did he." His calloused fingers bedazzled her naked skin. "I didn't just pull out that marriage bit spur of the minute. I been thinking on it, but I wanted to wait till summer. See, Janie'll be home from school then, and they can go to the farm; Hazel's folks have a farm up-country. I thought it would be easier for her, in among her own. Anyways, that's what I thought."

"Whatever you say."

"Hazel's always used me good. She's used the kids good. I don't want to dinge her more than I have to."

"I would've been content to go on as we were."

"I know you would've."

"She must be wondering why you're so late tonight."

"There's the good part of having a car like mine that's apt to break down anytime." He squeezed her rump. "Maybe I'll say the tail pipe come off."

She sat up and smiled at him.

He wrapped the blanket around her. "Why're you shivering?"

"Because I'm happy."

"Mighty contrary way to be happy." He pulled out his

handkerchief. "If you're crying now, you'll be a sopping mess at the wedding."

"Do we have to have a wedding?"

"A great big bash, with all them teachers and the photographer from the *Courier*. Everybody come to see Miss deVos marry the feller who cleans the toilets." He dried her eyes. "I bet you figured we'd sneak into City Hall when nobody wasn't looking."

She nodded.

"That's what we'll do then." He opened her blanket, and caressed her as he spoke, as though he hoped his caress could express things better than he. "I'm getting the best part of the bargain, a nice little shack with a Franklin stove, all new painted and shingled, a big yard for planting potatoes. We'll put in a garden, eh? You'd like that."

She slithered against him.

"It's mighty late," he said.

She was unbuttoning his shirt.

"I ain't got time for another one."

She was tugging down his pants.

"I got to start home." He was covering her with kisses.

"Good night," she said.

"See you Monday," he whispered, drawing her to him, pressing her closer.

The shock of joy which overwhelmed her surged unexpectedly . . . to pure relief.

This was her life. Not Clem's world, where she'd tried so hard to find her place, and couldn't . . . or what was worse, might have. Her world was here, where everything she did and said was okay.

"When we're married," he whispered, "I'll never have to leave you no more at night."

In that other world, she'd hated herself for being different. Here . . . was only tenderness for one another's great differences.

Words were lost in kisses. Thoughts collided. He moaned, or perhaps it was she . . . she could no longer tell. The awesome differences had melded them so completely together.

Hazel took the phone away from her right ear and switched it to the left. A person's ears got awful sore being on the phone all day and half the evening too. Land, it was nine o'clock already.

The calls begun while she was taking her bath, so she missed the first installment, but soon caught up with it, cause the story was repeated so many times she knew it by heart: Stella Deckety's cousin who lived in Town had a neighbor whose daughter-in-law helped out in one of them houses up on College Hill whenever they threw a party. The party was last Friday night, which means it took five days to get from the daughter-in-law to the neighbor to Stella Deckety's cousin to Fingabog Siding: Bliss Dawson was to be married to Miss Leona deVos.

Her Bliss. Leaving her for that long bone of a woman. She couldn't figure it backwards, forwards or sideways, and she was dizzy from trying to hammer it out while keeping one eye to the movie and listening in on the telephone, where tongues was going like the clapper on a cowbell.

Mrs. Sheehan and Lois Peaks was chewing it over now.

"They say it's been going on for almost a year."

"Well, you figure it, Lois. When did Bliss start working nights?"

"That was last May. I remember cause it was the week young Dave, Nora's friend, got his license suspended."

"So May to March. Almost a year."

"It might have started long before that though."

"True. It could have been brooding."

"They say he's crazy for her. Takes her dancing to Sun Luck Garden every night of the week, wrastling, up to the K-Mart, buys her everything."

"I heard he bought her a color TV for Christmas."

"One for each of them, eh?"

"Only you can be sure he was more careful to remember the payments on hers."

"She wouldn't have taken it sitting down like poor Hazel if they barged into her mansion and hauled the TV out."

"I guess she's quite a looker."

"Harry says her picture was in the *Courier* once or twice, but I can't recall it."

The two-way conversation suddenly became three-way; June broke in. "Didn't you see her? She was up to Sourgrass last year for the fair."

"No, I never seen her."

"Sure you did," insisted June. "She took young Janie on the Ferris wheel."

"I seen Janie on the Ferris wheel, but not with Miss deVos. She was up with some old-maid cousin visiting with the Carters."

"That wasn't no cousin of the Carters. That was Leona deVos."

"Couldn't of."

"It was. I heard Janie talk about her."

"She said that was Miss deVos?"

"Yes."

"Could be she went by the name of deVos."

"No, it was the same one; Janie said, *Miss deVos, who my father works for.*"

"That gangling great beanpole up on the Ferris wheel with Janie?"

"You seen her."

"Well, Lord love us."

"That beats all," said Mrs. Sheehan.

"It just goes to show," said Lois Peaks.

"What?"

"You know, about the book and the cover."

"She did have nice teeth."

"I noticed that."

"Real nice small white teeth."

There was a silence, then Lois offered hesitantly, "You might almost say she was pretty."

"Well, in one way."

June cut in. "You really couldn't say it."

"I guess you couldn't."

"Not pretty."

"You could say nice teeth."

"That's about all you could say."

"What was she doing on the wheel with Janie?"

"That's the question."

"What do you think?"

"Could be she wanted a ride."

"Don't be so ignorant."

"What would she want with little Janie?"

"Maybe distracting her."

"Why would she want to distract little Janie?"

"So she could go off with Bliss."

"How could she go off with Bliss when she was up with Janie?"

"There must be something in it."

"Oh, I guess."

"Heard about her house?" asked June.

"The mansion?"

"It ain't just a mansion."

"No?"

"It's got a pastorale," said June.

"It does!" said Lois.

"I didn't catch that," said Mrs. Sheehan.

"Pastorale, like they got in the back of Sun Luck, up on the wall."

"That painted paper?"

"Only more-so."

"Where's she got it?"

"Over her tub."

"Wouldn't she steam it up when she takes her bath?"

"She doesn't appear to."

"Could be she puts plastic over it."

"More than likely."

"And another pastorale over the boots."

"Seems to me the steam would go right through the plastic."

"And a soda fountain."

"A soda fountain! Wouldn't Bliss go for that now. He always had an awful sweet tooth."

"And a garbage-eater, dishwasher, anything you can think of."

"And there's poor Hazel washing dishes into the sink."

"I guess Hazel's taking it pretty hard," suggested Lois.

"Is she, June?" asked Mrs. Sheehan.

"I haven't exactly seen her. Since."

"That's a sign."

"I was talking to one of her cousins," said Lois, "lives over Nekedee."

"What's her opinion?"

"She seen it coming for ages."

"How so?"

"Four years ago, they was up to a wedding, and Hazel made a comment."

"What did she say?"

"She don't recall. But it signified at the time."

"You think it's been going on four years?"

"Bliss been up to the college for five."

"Could be it's going on five."

"He's only been working nights since last May."

"Many's the chance without working."

"Maybe the working merely clinched it."

"Stella Deckety's cousin's neighbor's daughter-in-law said they have terrible rows, fighting up and down the college, makes no odds who sees them."

"And Bliss such a quiet fellow."

"Never raises his voice to Hazel."

"Don't care enough to, I guess."

"They say he knocked her down and blackened her eye right out on Alling Street, with the whole world watching."

"Bliss Dawson?"

"Sure don't sound like him."

"Knocked her down, did he?"

"Blackened her eye. The blood was running all over Alling Street."

"Oh, he's crazy for her, all right."

"They say the beating he give her would have finished a smaller woman."

"I never knew Bliss to drink."

"That's because of Hazel being Pentecostal. But when he gets with the other one, he's just like a fish in water, drinking, fighting, causing ructions all over Alling Street."

"I thought of something!" said June.

"What's that?"

"Hazel told me the woman who cleans for Miss deVos comes from over Mactigouche. Don't you have some relation over Mactigouche?"

"Harry's cousin Edwina lives over Mactigouche."

"She'd know who it would be."

"Land, the woman who cleans! What she wouldn't know wouldn't be worth hearing."

"Can you call Edwina now?"

"All right. One, two, three, hang up."

Hazel put down the phone. She could save her ears on that one; she made up that woman over Mactigouche herself, one time when she was telling June about the mansion.

She grabbed a bag of potato chips and turned up the sound on the TV.

"*Our investigators have done a thorough job, Mrs. Bates.*"

"*Let me see the photographs.*"

The main thing was he wouldn't take her by surprise; that give her the upper crust. She ripped open the bag, stuffed her mouth as she walked back and forth.

Oh Lord, there was his car driving up.

Her stomach turned. He was in the shed.

"Lo, Hazel."

"Hello, Bliss." She went over to him and put her face up.

"Eh?"

"Ain't you going to kiss me?"

". . . Boys, I'm beat."

"You must've worked hard tonight."

"Is there anything to eat?"

She handed him the bag of chips.

He stuck a handful in his mouth.

"Don't your lady friend feed you?"

His mouth stopped mid-crunch.

"I know all about it, Bliss!"

He put down the chip bag.

"Everything! I know everything!"

"Then I guess I don't have to explain nothing."

"Is that all you got to say?"

"I'm sorry, Hazel."

"Sorry!" She spat out her words. "That you made me the talk of Fingabog Siding! That everybody from here to Nekedee knows how you been cheating on me while I been thinking you're out working every night!"

"I never wanted for you to get it that way. I was going to tell you myself."

"What was you going to tell me?" She raised her voice. "That you're walking out? That you're leaving me for that rangy schoolteacher tramp!"

"Ain't no need to 'smirch Leona."

"Ain't there!" she shouted. "I'll 'smirch her up and down the county and tell everyone who'll listen that she's a no-good piece of trash who whores off other women's husbands and . . ."

He grasped her arms.

"Don't you touch me, Bliss! Don't you hit me like you do that slut from the college! I'm your lawful wife, who you took in the eyes of God, for better or for worse"—her voice rose like the siren on an ambulance—"for richer or for poor, for sickness or for health, to take care of till death do us part, and you blasphemed your vows, you and your hussy, your filthy garbage . . ." She stopped for breath. "What are you doing at the dresser?"

"Packing my gear."

"No you ain't!" she hollered. "I ain't going to let you leave me! I ain't going to let you abandon them that needs you!"

She ran into the children's room and grabbed Joey from his crib. "This is your baby, Bliss!"

She yanked Janie out of her sleep, dragging her from the room by her pajamas.

"These are your children who need you!"

Janie's eyes bulged out of her head, and Joey started to wail.

"You can't leave us," bellowed Hazel.

Janie pulled free from her mother's grasp and flung herself at Bliss's legs. "Daddy, you ain't going to leave us!"

"You ain't going to leave us," screeched Hazel, "me and Janie and Joey!"

Joey let out a howl.

"Daddy, Daddy," screamed Janie, "please don't leave us, Daddy!"

"We're your family, Bliss!"

"What will we do without you?" cried Janie, banging her head against his stomach. "Please, Daddy, please!"

Hazel shook Joey in front of him. "Look at your son, Bliss!"

"Daddy, Daddy, Daddy!"

There was a rushing sound.

"Janie's peeing herself," shouted Hazel.

"No I'm not," screamed Janie. Her pajamas darkened, and a puddle was forming on the floor. "I didn't pee myself, Daddy! Please, Daddy, please. I didn't mean it, Daddy! I promise, please, I'll be good. I'll never do it again. I'll be a good girl from now on. Don't leave us, Daddy. I'm sorry. I'm sorry. I didn't mean it."

He lifted her in his arms.

"You'll get all wet," warned Hazel.

"I'll be so good, Daddy. I'm sorry. I never meant it. I

promise. From now on. Please. Daddy. Don't leave us." Her words were drowned in heavy breathing, and her body began to twitch, kicking against her father.

"Hazel, get a spoon!"

"Oh, Lord!" Hazel stuck Joey in the rocker and ran for a spoon.

Bliss separated Janie's teeth.

Her eyes were completely white.

"Call the doctor!"

"You call him!" Hazel wrenched Janie out of his arms. The little girl's skin was hot and wet, and her head and limbs were jerking. "My baby, my Janie!"

Bliss picked up the telephone. "I got to get through to the doctor. Would you please hang up. . . . Operator, get me the doctor . . . any doctor . . ."

"You see what you done!"

"Shut up, Hazel, I can't hear!"

"See what you done with your carryings-on and selfish ways!"

"Hello. Can you come to Fingabog Siding? My little girl. She's having convulsions."

"You done it, Bliss! You and your sinning!"

"Dawson. Fingabog Siding. No, she's seven."

"If Janie dies, you done it!"

"What's that? I can't hear you . . ."

"You done it, Bliss! The two of you!"

"Hazel, take off her clothes."

"Oh, my Janie!" She held the child down on the table, and took off her wet pajamas.

"The second house after the church."

"You done it now, Bliss Dawson, with your selfish adulterous ways!"

He hung up the phone.

"She's burning her life up, Bliss!"

"Jesus Christ, Hazel, stop it."

"It's His retribution!"

He filled a basin with water and took it to the table, then lifted his daughter's limp arm and rubbed it gently between his hands.

The day was windy, but it was a soft spring wind, working with the sun to melt the snow and bring the frost up from the earth, along with the crocuses Bliss had set out last September.

She turned right on Alling Street. They would walk to work together and walk back home together and the changing seasons would be the cycles of her happiness.

Night would be his warmth and day his voice. She turned right again on Sussex, aware that she was as balmy as the balmy wind, but what did it matter. Bliss had promised to live with her.

The gates of the university glittered black in the sun, and all his lovely mundane ways lay before her like unopened presents; she joined the students marching up the hill to classes—sensible, strait-laced Associate Professor deVos, high as a kite behind her Scottish tweed facade. There'd be his lunch pail on the counter and his coarse clothing in the closet and weekends locked in love.

She climbed the stairs to her office, thinking not of her first class, but of Bliss's ears, which she'd grown to adore, because they were so touching, sticking out exuberantly.

She turned the corner to her office.

He was standing in front of her door, facing it.

She could see only his back and the droop of his limbs, but it was enough. The listless angle of his shoulders, the grim tilt of his cap, the wretched way he stood before the door brought the castle of her gladness crumbling down around her. She turned and bolted.

He thundered after her.

She ran down the stairs, but he was beside her. "I got to talk to you."

She nodded, and they trudged up to the parking lot, her big galoshes dragging in the slush. It was over. As she'd always known. The man walking beside her in the knit cap was someone she'd asked to help her change a light bulb; the rest had been a dream.

"I know you got classes, but I ain't got much time."

In the dream, he'd said she would soon have all his time. In the dream, they were two halves who'd come together at last, but she should have known there was no other half for a monstrosity like her.

They were standing at a car which was blue on top and red below.

"Get in."

She stumbled into the car; he drove, down through the old university buildings, down through maple trees running with sap, past the snow melting in gorges on frozen lawns.

"A man can't always think of just himself." He steered

through the gates. "He has to think about them that needs him."

Through the windshield the sun blazed in, hurting her eyes. "Janie and Joey . . ."

Sussex Avenue was crowded with rush-hour traffic. "They're just little kids, just . . ."

There was Alling Street. "Some kids takes things harder than others. . . ."

She looked through the window at two cats fighting in the snow, standing on their hind legs with their paws about each other.

"I'm going to get a new job, see. It shouldn't be too hard, a man like me with fourteen trades."

They turned down Farrier Lane.

"Digging, plumbing, carpentry, masonry, tractors . . ."

He was rattling on, and she could hardly understand him, but each word tore another piece out of her nature, carrying it off on the warm spring wind.

"Worst comes to worst, I can go back to the woods. A feller can always work cutting down trees. I still got my chain saw, even if it ain't the best no more. . . ."

She needed some air; she got out of the car and stood in the path.

She heard him get out beside her.

He was looking at the shack.

She turned away from him. Why had he come to tell her these things about jobs and children? Why had he come to hollow her out with his words?

Suddenly she heard a noise, like the Bluebird's engine when it wouldn't start in winter.

She turned to the car.

The sound wasn't coming from there.

Something was trying to break free in Bliss, but an obstruction held it back, allowing him only this harsh, helpless sound.

She put her arms around him.

"Never mind," she murmured.

"Fine comfort to you I am," he said hoarsely, wiping his eyes with his sleeve.

They went inside.

The morning light through the tiny squares of windowpane patterned the room with a dozen frames of brightness.

They stood in the dazzling warmth, and the sunlight was so strong on him, and he and she so utterly real, it was unthinkable that there should be anything else for them.

She reached to the window to draw back the last narrow ruffle of curtain. He caught her wrist, and pulled the curtains closed. They moved like sleepwalkers to the bed.

Even emptiness, she thought, held desire; or maybe it was habit; or sadness flowering.

His fingers moved slowly, removing her clothes, and she wished they would move more slowly, in ever slower increments of time, ever dividing, until time had been trapped in his fingers.

"If I met you before," he said, lying on top of her, "if I met you when you first come here, before I was married."

But it was easier not to speak, to pretend there was nothing between them but flesh, to let the flowering have its way as the sun traveled over the house.

"Ten or fifteen years," he said, "they'll be growed up. Ten or fifteen years, they won't need me. We'll only be forty-five, fifty. Still in our prime, eh?"

She didn't answer.

"That old teacher of yours. We'll be younger than him." He held her tight against him. "You think it's just talk. It ain't just talk."

They got dressed in the early afternoon light, and walked together to the car.

"I won't be seeing you no more."

"I know."

"I'm giving notice, see. I'm going to get another job."

"You told me about it."

"I know I told you about it!" He shook her. "Why don't you fight me! Make me say the hell with them!"

"I don't know how," she sobbed.

He patted her softly. "I got to go now."

She watched him get into his car.

He rolled down the window as though to tell her something, then rolled it up again and drove away.

The lane was empty. No one ever drove down it but Bliss.

She walked up the path to her shack, where she lived by herself.

Hazel threw a party to set the record straight. Not a big bash, just June and Mabel, cozy-like over tea and a fresh batch of donuts.

"It's a much better job," she said, pouring for her guests. "He don't exactly do the building himself, he brings the nails, holds the boards up and such. It ain't that he couldn't do more, but being he only has sixth-grade education, he don't qualify for the union. Them carpenters are real strict. Not like that old maintenance crew."

"It suits him, does it?" Mabel gummed her donut.

"To a hair."

"That's all that matters then," said June. "A man has to be happy in his work."

They munched in silence, with Young Tony Andrews flickering black and white before them.

When Easy Credit come and took the color set again, Bliss said there wasn't no money for to get it back and that was the all of it. She was ready to lay into him—but she seen a look across his face, as if he was wondering where he was, and it give her an odd turn, like maybe that idea he had to pack his gear was still festering in his brain. So she didn't throw no row, nor suggest no evening work. She could bide her time in black and white till things was more normal-like.

"I'm glad to hear them rumors wasn't true," said Mabel, "about the college firing Bliss."

Hazel snorted.

"They really should have fired her," said June, "instead of Bliss. She ain't got no family to support."

"I ain't sure who you're referring to," said Hazel.

"She means Miss deVos," explained Mabel.

"Oh, that teacher who Bliss did a little work for. I clear forgot her name."

Mabel shook her head. "A pretty face can lead the best man astray."

They turned back to the story. Poor Young Tony Andrews was suffering something fierce over breaking with his new woman.

"This is an awful good batch of donuts."

"Have another."

"Thank you."

"Avery seen some crocuses in front of City Hall."

"They're always a month earlier in Town than what we are," said Mabel.

"Bliss is usually the first to spot them. Funny he never mentioned it."

"You going to Alva's paint-on–embroidery party?" asked June.

"Wednesday night, ain't it?"

"Wednesday this week, but the lady from Town said she'd make it to suit our convenience after she sees the kind of turnout.' "

"I can sit Wednesday night," offered Mabel.

"Bliss can sit."

"The bedspread kit costs fifty dollars." June chewed her donut. "But that's including sixteen tubes of paint."

"And the lady from Town don't charge for the lessons?"

"Not so far as Alva knows."

"What else do they got besides the bedspread kit?"

"Tablecloth, tea towels, pot holders, pillow slips."

"Is most everyone taking the bedspread kit?"

"I imagine." June got up to separate Donny and Joey, who were gouging at each other's face in the playpen.

"Two smart little fellers," said Mabel.

Young Donny appeared to be toeing out.

"I been meaning to ask you, Hazel." June sat back in her chair. "What was the name of that woman over Mactigouche?"

"What woman would that be?"

"The one who cleans for Miss deVos."

"Now how would I know a thing like that?"

Mabel brushed the crumbs from her chin. "What I always say is bygones be bygones. No point in raking embers when there ain't no more bread in the oven."

"I'm sure you told me her name once."

"I'm sure I forgot if I ever did."

The door burst open. "Hello, Granny Mabel."

"Take off your boots! They're thick with mud."

"Hello, Janie." Mabel peered toward the door.

June looked at her watch. "Time for me to get Avery's supper started."

"And I got to start Bliss's."

"My daddy comes home for supper," said Janie.

The women stood.

"Come back again."

"We're going home, Donny." June pulled her son off Joey's face.

"Can I have a donut, Mommy?"

"You'll spoil your appetite."

"Come visit me sometime, Janie." Mabel groped her way out through the shed. The door closed behind them.

"Can I help you make Daddy's supper?"

"You can clean off the table."

Janie picked up two cups and saucers. "We have to make Daddy a real good supper so he'll always want to come home to us."

Wham, on the head. *Whop*, on the ear.

Janie dropped the dishes.

"Get into your pajamas! You're going to bed right now!"

Janie scurried into her room.

Hazel bent over the floor and swept up the broken pieces. Only three cups left into the set; she supposed that one of these days, Bliss'd have to take her up to the K-Mart to buy them there new Jasmine dishes.

The night was moonless, but the stars made up for it, dazzling the darkness of the sleeping town.

She made for the river.

By the end of the week, it would flood; it was already rising. The benches along the embankment were just above the water line. They would be covered, along with the trash cans and the picnic table by the fish-and-chips stand.

Starlight shimmered white on the water.

He was bending over his shovel, his skin gleaming like milk in the noontime sun.

Waves gently lapped the shore, stirring old longings for death and nothingness. How simple it would be to get up and walk in and let the icy water fill her lungs and numb her flesh. *The rough hair of his thighs brushed against her as they rocked. "That's where I'm happy, Leona, see."*

Starlight danced on the river. She reached down and touched it. The stream would quickly take her, and no one would ever miss her.

In the glow of the Franklin stove, his pale eyes shone on her like a mirror.

She would never again see his face beside the fire, the beauty of his shoulders, the muscles of his arms and chest, like supple, polished wood.

"Come up here, Leona." He scooped her in his arms.

She nestled beside him on the pillow.

"Tell me something," he demanded.

His voice fell like a stone on the water, repeating itself in dark rings, spreading out and out, until it was gone.

She rose from the bench, and started up the street. There was no forever. There was only one step after the other, the monotony of her days, the motions of existence, the pinch of her fashionable shoes—that's what she'd concentrate on, shuffling along the streets, one step after the other, drowning her years in little things.

Music and laughter floated from the Chiassons' house. She hesitated at the foot of the stairs, feeling like a night-flying creature who senselessly drifts toward the lights of civilization. She might beat her wings against the panes; she might even enter the bright place.

"Leona!"

"Dolly!" But it was a mistake, she knew that, trailing behind her hostess, alighting in the midst of the perfume and the chatter.

"You're just being cruel, Arthur . . ."

". . . I hear it ran into five figures."

"Actually, I suspect . . ."

". . . soundproofed the entire upstairs."

237

"Chuck Chiasson's into . . ."

". . . perhaps he'll have a stroke."

"Why Chuck! Yes, I would like another."

"In between Reich and Janov . . ."

". . . re-experiencing the original trauma."

"Doesn't it seem . . ."

The voices tinkled, touched.

He leaned on his shovel and smiled.

The pain ripped through her.

"Deirdre was into something quite similar."

"She sat around in nothing but diapers for a week."

"It sounds traumatic."

"I believe she retained her brassiere."

It was a lovely movie, all about the desert and this Englishman who fell in with some Arabs. Land, he was handsome, fair hair and glittery eyes.

"The sort of thing a person ought to see in color." She sort of threw that out to the room.

Look at them camels, would you! Humpty-dumpting along.

Bar-B-Que potato chips got her gums sore after a while. "Would you send over them regular chips."

The bag landed in her lap.

Commercial.

She turned to the table, where Bliss sat staring at his cigarette.

"What you moping about?"

"I ain't moping."

"You are."

"Just smoking."

She bit her hangnail off. He had that festering look on his face again, like he was trying to figure something. "Lois Peaks's husband got her a new bedroom suit."

He kept on smoking.

"Dresser, bedstead, highboy, genuine distressed-walnut finish, eighteen dollars a month, that's with the trade-in on their old suit." He wasn't listening; she raised her voice. "Mattress, box spring . . ."

"Daddy!"

Bliss stubbed his butt, and went to the children's room.

That Janie! Hazel turned back to the TV. Almost every night now, waking up with nightmares. More a way to get attention than anything else.

This was an awful long movie, so much sand.

She got up and took her nightgown out of the dresser, listening to the voices in the other room.

"He was woolly, see, like a lamb."

Same old stories.

She took off her clothes. Fat. She couldn't deny it, hurrying into her nightgown.

She sat down on their couch.

The handsome Englishman whirled on the desert.

Bliss still hadn't come back to her. Not like a husband.

She sighed, settling herself in the pillows. Maybe he would tonight.

Sooner or later he had to.

A man couldn't hold it inside forever.